FENNER

George Harmon Coxe

G.K.HALL &CO.

 Boston, Massachusetts

1971

Library of Congress Cataloging in Publication Data

Coxe, George Harmon, 1901-

Fenner.

Large print ed.
I. Title.
[PZ3.C83942Fe3] [PS3505.09636] 813'.5'2 77-38102
ISBN 0-8161-6003-1 (1.print)

Published in Large Print by arrangement
with Alfred A. Knopf, Inc.

Set in Photon 18 pt Times Roman

For

JANET *again*

1

She had been an inmate — or was she more properly classified as a patient? — for two weeks. Thirteen days to be exact. And out on the secondary highway to the city now, she looked back and tried to count the buildings in the complex that was the State Hospital at Ufford.

She had decided even before she left to avoid the Thruway, which ran a quarter of a mile directly in front of her building, because the area between was too open. She would have been conspicuous and easily spotted. Because she had been given a parole pass — awarded to those chosen few thought to be sufficiently rational and trustworthy — two days before, she had felt free to wander along the edge of the recreation fields, past the older buildings at the rear, and up the wooded slope until she came finally to the old road, now used by those who wished to avoid the toll.

Luckily she had a decent dress of tailored navy wool, stockings, and good blue shoes with sensible heels. For the outfit supplied by the state for those who had no money or nowhere to go would be a dead giveaway to any motorist remotely familiar with the institutional uniform — a cheap cotton print, styleless and ill fitting; short white sox and bare legs instead of stockings; sneakers or sandals of some kind for their shuffling gait.

She had walked for another quarter of a mile along the edge of the macadam before looking for a lift. Only two cars passed her; another sped by from the opposite direction. Now, glancing over her shoulder, she decided it was time to use her thumb.

Two more sedans with couples in the front seat passed her, the men curious-eyed. The next one stopped. Two men in working clothes this time. They pulled up just ahead and a window rolled down as she came abreast.

"You want a lift lady?"

In their thirties, she thought, needing shaves. But it was not their overall unattractiveness that decided her. Beggars couldn't be choosers, but there was something about their grins, the sly lascivious glints in their eyes that bothered her. Or was it just her imagination, coupled with the growing fear of discovery?

"I'm just going to the next house." She pointed. "To use the phone."

"Sure?" Some disappointment here, or was it suspicion?

"Quite sure. But thank you anyway."

"Okay. Suit yourself, sister."

Grins gone now, shrugging somehow, they drove off with quick acceleration.

A hundred yards farther along she heard another car behind her, this time with the full-throated sound of a truck diesel, and when a backward glance confirmed her guess she stopped and half-lifted one hand. Truck drivers were supposed to be helpful and courteous, weren't they? Especially if they worked for a reputable company with a fleet?

As it slowed and stopped just ahead she had only a glimpse of the driver, her angle of vision hiding everything but his head. Not a tractor-trailer type, but good-sized, dual tires at the rear, and an aluminum van with a company identification that said Bayside Trucking. Then the door swung open and she was peering into the elevated cab at a stocky, black-browed man, this one clean-shaven and not bad looking.

"Trouble?"

Once again she hesitated, but not for long. It was not that she was entirely reassured by the driver's appearance or possible motives. Vaguely remembered stories of assaulted hitch-hikers suggested caution. The trouble was, she was running out of time. If she passed up this chance, how long before anything better came along?

For she was convinced that they were already looking for her back at Ufford. The last time she had glanced at her watch it had been after four. And four was one of the appointed hours for mandatory medication. She could hear the call now as it bounced off the corridor walls: "Medication ladies!" Very loud, it was. Demanding too.

Then the quick-forming lines just as it was in the cafeteria. And the nurses in their glass-enclosed station, with their check lists and the trays of paper cups with pills and

4

capsules, small handfuls some of them, to be gulped instantly and washed down with a swallow or two of water.

She could almost hear them calling. "Where is Carol Browning?" No, not quite like that. From the very first day you had only your given name. "Where's Carol?" That's what they'd say.

Within minutes they'd know she wasn't on that floor, and since each floor was locked they'd also know she wasn't in that building. Then the telephones would ring in other stations and the guards and other hospital personnel would comb the grounds. By now the State Police and the local police in nearby towns would have been notified...

"A little," she said to the waiting driver. "I could use a lift."

"Sure, hop in."

The first step was high, but her skirt was too short to hamper her; then she was perched on the wide seat cushion as the man levered the door shut and the automatic transmission took over. Only now did she realize how tired she was and she gave into it, grateful, aware of nothing beyond the windshield.

5

Safe now, at least for a little while, she let her thoughts slide back over the recent past and the experience she had been through. Nothing could diminish the anger and resentment she felt for the husband who had put her there, but she had been fortunate to draw one of the modern buildings, and when she was able to think rationally once more she had to admit the hall and rooms were clean, the bathrooms well kept, the recreational facilities adequate.

Even the food was good. Unlike the other place she had been in Connecticut, where you had linen tablecloths and fresh flowers each day for decoration, Ufford needed the efficiency of a cafeteria system, but the food was reasonably tasty and well prepared. The nurses were both capable and understanding and yet, for the occasional obstreperous few, they had the firmness and resolution to handle each situation quickly and well.

Of course she could never get used to the ward idea. No room of your own, five or more roommates with their often slovenly habits, and the night sounds and the disappearance of small things like lipsticks should you be careless enough to leave them around . . .

"What?" she said, her mind jerked back to the present by some unanswered question.

"I said, did your car break down?"

Oh, Lord, she thought. *What do I say so he won't suspect I walked away from Ufford? Or does he already think so?*

Aware somehow, without looking at him, that he had been studying her, conscious, it seemed, of glances that were evaluating her legs and the tightness of the skirt across her thighs, she said: "Out of gas, of all the stupid things."

"I didn't see your car."

"On that last side road. I knew I'd never get a lift there—"

"Why not the Thruway?"

"I remembered the no-hitchhiking signs."

"Yeah, that's right. The state cops'll pick you up for that. So you want to be dropped at the nearest filling station?"

"Well, no," she said, and was surprised how easily the rest came. "It's my husband's fault for not putting enough gas in yesterday. Let him come and get it. Serve

7

him right . . . How far do you go?"

"Somerville."

"Would it be awfully out of your way if you went through Cambridge?"

"Not that far out. That where you live?"

"No, but I can get the subway from the Square."

Not until she put the thought into words did it occur to her with some odd and sickening sense of shock that she could not even do that. She didn't have the fare. She was, in fact, penniless. What money she'd had had been taken by the nurses when she was admitted and doled out for certain little luxuries from time to time. You had to ask for a dime to make a collect phone call and then you had to give it back.

She was still very much aware of his almost continuous, corner-of-the-eye surveillance. But then men had looked at her like that since she had been in her middle teens, sometimes with open admiration, sometimes with other things in mind. She was aware that she had been blessed with a good figure; she would be twenty-five next Tuesday and everything was still in the right place. At five-seven in bare feet, she was not too tall to stand straight and walk with pride. Her skin was good, even without makeup, and her medium-blond hair was natural, some of the strands still bleached by the summer sun now in mid-October.

No, it wasn't the man's look that bothered her, it was the thought that, one way or another, she was going to ask him for money. She not only needed subway fare but a change of clothes. Fortunately she knew of a secondhand boutique where she might pick up some used things . . .

A new urgency checked such thoughts as she realized the town they were passing through was Watertown. They would be in Cambridge in fifteen minutes. She had that much time and so, gathering her courage, she came right out with it.

"Could you lend me some money?"

The reaction to the request was sudden and unexpected. The laugh came loudly with a connotation that reminded her of an out-and-out leer. The sound jarred her and brought with it the first touch of irritation.

"Did I say something funny?"

"You sure did, honey. I fell for that line

twice a long time ago but those chicks were better actresses. The sob story came first. Like this. You lost your purse, or someone snatched it. It had your return ticket to Bangor or New York or Jersey City and if I can just let you have enough for bus fare and a meal you'll mail it right back to me, with interest yet."

He turned to her then, ignoring the traffic, dark stare challenging and humorless now.

"You know something. I don't think there was any car. I think you're running from Ufford."

"In a hundred-and-fifty-dollar dress?"

"Why not? Not all those inmates are state wards, or whatever you call 'em."

His sudden challenge, the open scorn in the voice, fanned her irritation into something akin to loathing and she thought, *All right, mister. I'll talk your language if that's how it has to be.*

"If I did run away, you're in trouble!"

"I am?"

"For aiding or abetting — or whatever the phrase is — an escapee. You knew I ran away and yet you drove me thirty miles to help me make it. Talk yourself out of that and you'll still be out of a job for picking up a hitchhiker. I've heard *that's* against most company rules."

That got a quick burst of profanity before he said: "I could dump you now, sister. It would be your word against mine and they know you're a nut or you wouldn't be in Ufford."

"Dump me?" She laughed at him. "Here in this traffic with me screaming my head off? Try it!"

It took him perhaps three silent minutes to digest her threat. She tried to help him along, rationalizing now.

"I'm Mrs. George Browning," she said and gave him her address. "You can come looking for me if I don't mail you the money. What's your name?"

"Fred Megan."

"Where do you live?"

"Uh-unh. You think I want you lousing things up with my wife? You want to get in touch with me, try the office. Bayside Trucking . . . How much did you have in mind?"

"Ten dollars."

"Ten!" He eyed her scornfully. "You don't fool, do you? You got anything—I mean, like collateral? Just to prove you're leveling?"

She glanced down at her wristwatch, not the platinum and diamond one, a round sports watch. It was a good one, but she assumed that there must be imitations that probably could be bought for ten or fifteen dollars. Then, her eyes straying, she saw the wedding ring.

Platinum and studded with small diamonds that completely encircled it except for a small place where the date was engraved. George Browning had slipped it on her finger nearly three years ago but she had paid for it; eighteen hundred at Lowe & Company. She slipped it off and he took it.

"Nice," he said. "Rhinestones?"

"Do they sell rhinestones at Lowe & Company?"

He was turning it over in his stubby fingers, one eye on the road. Then, leaning forward, he held it with only the edge protruding between thumb and forefinger. This he put against the glass of an instrument gauge and made a hard, downward dash. She could just about see the frosty little scratch but it was there.

"Okay," he said, and this time there was a touch of admiration in his grin. "You're a tough broad."

She looked right at him, her small smile tight and mirthless. "You bring it out in a girl. May I have the ten?"

He felt for a worn black wallet, handed it to her. She found a ten among the bills and held it up so he could see it. They were crossing the Charles now with the Square a few blocks ahead.

"Somebody will phone you and tell you where to bring the ring," she said. "Maybe tomorrow. You can pick up your ten along with something extra for your time and cab fare."

This time he shook his head, the grin still there. The small grunt that followed carried an inflection of doubt and resignation.

"A real tough broad," he said. "Do you always order people around like that? I mean you sound like you've had a lot of practice."

"Only when I have to, Fred," she said sweetly but with some small sense of

13

triumph. "Anywhere near the Square will be fine for me."

2

The smallish four-storied building just around the corner from Boylston where Jack Fenner had his office was a somewhat ancient structure that had been made more presentable by sand-blasting the facade and modernizing the interior. The entrance foyer had been neatly redone and a modest automatic elevator had replaced the creaking grilled cage.

The pebbled-glass door on the left side of the third floor corridor bore two names to indicate a suite. Reading from the top the lettering said: J. H. FENNER. Underneath was FRANK QUINN. In smaller lettering: *Attorney at Law*.

There was, in fact, a suite. In terms of class and yearly rental it was several notches above the shabby one-room place Fenner had rented when he went in business for himself some years back. The walls of the anteroom were paneled—real wood but veneer and not solid all the way through. There was a good green carpet, an imitation-leather sofa, and four chairs with seats of matching material. A black coffee table with reasonably current copies of *Look, Life,* and *Sports Illustrated;* plenty of ashtrays, and drum lamps on the two end tables.

It was five thirty on this Wednesday afternoon—a half hour later than he had planned—when Fenner walked in to find an unexpected visitor. Recognition, even in profile, was instantaneous but that this might be a potential client never occurred to him. Alice Maxwell was still at her desk in the half-glass, half-wood cubby that had been partitioned in one corner. He caught her eye at once and saw that she was about to speak, but the bare-headed man who had turned at his entrance beat her to it.

"Mr. Fenner? I'm George Browning."

"I know," said Fenner without enthusiasm.

"Yeah." The light-blue eyes were veiled but challenging, the chuckle sardonic. "I'll bet you do."

He was a big man, close to forty, soft-looking somehow but not really fat. His face was tanned, the blond wavy hair much too long for Fenner's taste; the slacks and the navy blazer with some club insignia on the breast pocket were expertly tailored, and Fenner, who knew something about such things, guessed that two hundred plus would be about right for the slacks and jacket.

Now, glancing at his wristwatch, Browning said: "I've been waiting nearly a half hour. Your secretary said you'd —"

"Sorry, I got held up." Fenner's abruptness was intentional because he knew too much about the man to like him.

"Okay, you're here." Browning gestured toward the open door of the inner office. "Can we go inside?"

Fenner motioned ahead of him and paused next to his secretary's cubby.

"There was someone else here before *he* came," she began but Fenner cut her off.

"It can wait, Alice. Can you stick it out a little longer? That is if you don't have a date."

"No date," she said and made a face.

"Jimmy's on nights this week."

"Oh, and is Frank still here? Will you ask him to wait a few minutes just in case?"

Browning had been inspecting the corner office which had been done over much like the outer room except that there was a well-filled bookcase and a heavy steel — fireproof, the dealer said — filing cabinet. Now he gave another indecipherable grunt and took the chair in front of the desk.

"Not bad," he said. "Business must be good for private investigators these days."

"For some," Fenner said flatly. "What's on your mind?"

"I understand you've done some work for my wife."

"Is that a question or a statement?"

"Oh, you won't be violating any confidence," Browning added airily. "She's the one who told me about you."

Fenner sat down and got a cigarette going, his dark-green eyes steady and his lean, angular face expressionless. He watched the other inspect the filing cabinet in the corner, listened as he continued.

"I suppose it's all there. Reports about me, I mean."

"Enough. Where you came from. How you happened to have a job on that dude ranch in Nevada where potential divorcees went to put in their residence requirements."

"She could have told you that."

"She did. What she really wanted to know was what you'd been doing lately."

Browning's sneer showed again. "You covered a lot of ground, didn't you? Must have cost Carol."

"I told her it would. She said she could afford it."

"Okay, Fenner. So tell me this—have you finished with her?"

"Yes."

"No further obligations?"

"Not in a business sense."

"Then will you work for me? I mean now?"

"Why me?"

"Because you did such a damn good job on me. Will you?"

"I might when I hear the rest of it. What have you got in mind?"

"It's nothing against Carol, in case you

feel some loyalty to her. In fact, you'll be helping her."

"It'll cost you. I'm expensive."

"How much?"

"Twenty bucks an hour."

That got attention. The insolent pose disappeared and Browning sat up, eyes wide with shock.

"Twenty bucks?" he said in wonderment. "An hour? Jesus, man, how many hours do you work a week?"

"Sometimes ten, sometimes eighty. You pay for what I do. When I use help you pay *their* rate. I can give you some names. A couple of these get ten an hour, some, good enough for a simple stake-out, you can get for five."

"No. I've no time. I told you this is urgent."

"I asked you before — why me?"

"Because you'd have to know Carol better than anyone else I could get."

"What do you want me to do?"

"Find her."

Fenner's gaze remained intent, but inside things were happening. He forgot to dislike this man and his quick concern was genuine, not from what was said but *how* it was said.

"You're still separated, aren't you? When did you see her last?"

"Sunday."

"So she decided to take a little trip. Why should she bother to tell you?"

Browning shook his head. "This was no trip. She *ran* away."

"From where?"

"Ufford. This afternoon. They missed her shortly after four."

Fenner heard the words distinctly. There was no mistaking their meaning, but it took a few seconds to digest them. This time it was his turn to stare.

"The State Hospital? Who sent her there?"

"I did. Me and Dr. Garic. He signed the commitment papers. She used to be a patient of his. I just happened to stop by her place a couple of weeks ago, luckily I guess, and she was out of her skull, seeing three of everything, insisting she could fly. She had the window open before I knew she must have flipped. I had a hell of a time. She's a big girl and strong. I called Garic, practically had to sit on her until he got there. You know she'd been away once before?"

Fenner did not bother to nod. Carol Browning had told him about those six weeks. But that had been mostly an alcoholic problem. Now, as the feeling of loathing grew in him, he tried to keep his voice even as he digressed.

"She'll be twenty-five next week. The trust she's been living on will be dissolved and paid over to her. I got the idea it would amount to between two and three million."

"So?"

"And you sent her to a *state* institution. That place in Connecticut she went to before was private."

"Sure. Like a country club. Beautiful grounds, gourmet meals. We figured—Garic thought it was worth a chance—that Ufford would shock her into realizing she had to straighten up and stay that way."

Fenner pushed his chair back, aware that such rationalization was possible but not quite believing it. He considered this man who was Carol's second husband and whose only income was the thousand-a-month

22

allowance she gave him after stopping all his charge accounts. He admitted there was a superficial handsomeness here that could appeal to many women. But what he saw now was the almost colorless eyes too small for the face, the squarish jaw with the small mouth that could so easily turn mean.

To avoid looking at him he stood up and walked to the widow, a lean, wiry-looking man a bit under six feet. The thinning black hair seemed to accentuate the angularity of his face and he combed it flat from the part to make the window's peak more prominent. Except for the eyes, which were quick, observant, and seldom still, he did not fit the image of his profession. The gray worsted-flannel slacks, the well-cut Shetland jacket, and the polished wing-type black shoes would have been more in place on State Street or in some advertising office.

When he was ready he went back to his desk, still churning inside but his manner at once businesslike.

"Okay, Browning. She walked away before four this afternoon?"

"Right. They say they gave her a parole

pass yesterday because they thought she was okay. That gave her the freedom of the grounds. They phoned me when they couldn't find her, notified the State Police. Garic too. He says—"

"She could be anywhere by now. She's got money."

"No money."

"What do you mean no money? You didn't leave her up there—"

"The nurses take any money and hand it out a quarter at a time. She didn't have a dime."

Fenner glanced at his watch. "The State Police and the local authorities must already be looking for her. If there's a bulletin out on her they could pick her up any time."

"I don't want that; neither would she."

And Fenner thought: *Neither would I*. As he hesitated, aware now of the other's sincerity, Browning said:

"I just figure that if you're good enough to charge the rates you do, maybe you can beat the police to it."

"Okay." Fenner leaned forward, his gaze flat and intent. "It's your dough and I'm available. You got a thousand in your bank account?''

''Well''—again the surprise showed—"just about."

"Write a check. What I don't earn you get back. I'll give you a receipt," he added and pulled a pad of blanks toward him.

The intercom buzzed as he signed the receipt. "Kent Murdock, Mr. Fenner," Alice said. "Will you talk to him?"

"Put him on. Hi, Kent. How're you doing, boy?"

"Jack." The familiar voice seemed unusually sober. "Can you come over to my place?"

"When?"

"Now, or as soon as you can make it?"

"You going to give me drinks and take me out to dinner?"

"Drinks, yes. No dinner. I need some help."

"Professional or otherwise?"

"You can decide when you get here." Then, as though Murdock had no intention of taking no for an answer: "If you've got a date stall it for a bit. When can you make it?"

The earnest intensity in his friend's voice told Fenner that whatever Murdock had in mind was important.

"A half hour if I'm lucky."

"Good. I'll have the ice and booze ready."

Fenner glanced at the check Browning had written, took out a coat wallet, slipped it inside, again pressed the intercom.

"Alice . . . Type out a simple to-whom-it-may-concern paragraph stating that the undersigned would appreciate any help that can be given to the bearer, who represents him. Mr. Browning can sign it on his way out."

Browning had resumed his slouch, but the small light-blue eyes were curious.

"What's that for?"

"Some people, especially doctors, get very evasive when you question them about their friends and patients. I'll want to talk to your man Garic; if we don't turn up your wife by morning I'll probably go out to Ufford and talk to some nurses and the doctor on her floor."

"You'll need some help."

"No problem. There's an organization called Guards Incorporated. Cops moonlighting, ex-cops. Much of the work is usually for added protection to large apartment buildings and housing complexes. But I've got a guy in the other office I can use for starters. A lawyer who has worked for me before and can use some extra dough. Your wife still has the same apartment?"

"And the house in Brookline. But that's been more or less closed up for some time. I'm at the University Club."

You also, Fenner thought, *have a little hideout for extracurricular projects not sanctioned by the University Club.* What he said was: "I know. I'll check with you when and if I get a lead."

He reached for the intercom, and when Alice Maxwell answered he said: "Mr. Browning is on his way out to sign that note."

He waited, his stare cold and deliberate until Browning hoisted himself from the chair. He started for the door, turned, his eyes narrowed and his irritation showing.

"You're a real snotty bastard, aren't you Fenner?"

"Some people think so." Fenner's tight

27

grin was malicious. "Others say I'm a very kind and compassionate individual. I'd like to help but I didn't send for you."

"All right, all right. Just do your job . . . Oh, yeah. And don't pad your expense account, hunh?"

3

Frank Quinn had made a series of mistakes a few years back. The first, the catalytic agent, that led to the second and third was innocent enough and wholly understandable. He just happened to fall in love and marry a pretty Irish-Catholic girl who had a full-blown body, a shrewish disposition, and a prissy attitude about sex.

A few years of this, along with certain scruples that prevented him from being comfortable sexually with a pro, eventually made his casual drinking a serious problem. When his wife finally left him the habit was still there, and with no incentive to change it, it remained so until, at thirty-seven, the future with one of the city's better law firms was no longer there. In his whisky-fogged brain one careless mistake led inevitably to points of law overlooked, slipshod preparations, uncertain handling of witnesses and evidence.

Religious beliefs prevented a divorce. There were no children. Now in his forties, still likable and well-known in city hall and courtroom corridors, he handled a wide variety of cases, most of them capably since they were usually routine and seldom very rewarding. Yet he was still convinced that the break would come — if not tomorrow or the next day, then next month or the one after. Somewhere, somehow, he would get the one case that would not only earn him the publicity he needed but a fat fee as well. Money was always a problem; he'd do what he had to get it, but it was this imaginary case just around the corner that was most important.

Fenner had known him casually when he was still married and understood something of what he had been through. Fenner had occasionally done some work for Quinn's former firm and was aware that the man had been more than adequate as an investigator on certain cases that had his personal attention. When the building where Fenner had his one-room office was demolished, Quinn had heard that Fenner was looking for new quarters and suggested they share them. That way, he'd argued, they could not only split expenses but possibly throw some business each other's way.

Fenner was thinking of this when Quinn opened the door, and he took no pleasure in the fact that he was the one who almost always did the hiring. He felt sorry for the man, but never in the slightest way did he let such thoughts show. This was one of those times when he could help because he had already decided that Browning could pay ten an hour for Quinn's services instead of getting someone from Guards Incorporated and paying five.

"Sit down Frank," he said. "Thanks for waiting."

"No problem."

Quinn settled himself, a chubby man with sallow skin, thinning hair, and tired eyes of washed-out blue.

"If you're free, or can get free, for a few hours tonight, I can get you ten."

Quinn's grin was spontaneous. "I can get free. It must be special at that price."

"Not special, a simple stake-out; it's you

that has the special knowledge this time. Do you remember Carol Browning? You must have met her. She was in frequently a while back."

"Do I? Hah!" Quinn's eyes came alive. "Tall, blond, built, rich, and exciting to look at. A little arrogant, or maybe it was just me."

Fenner nearly grinned at the exactness of the description but controlled the impulse and said: "You know where she lives?"

Quinn said he thought so and mentioned an address. "That small, old, expensive place next to the big new apartment."

Fenner nodded and gave the basics of the story Browning had told him. Quinn's reaction was much like Fenner's.

"Ufford?" he said. "With her money? What kind of a monster is he?"

Fenner ignored the comment. "Park across the street if you can, or any place where you can see the entrance. You'll recognize her?"

"Hell, yes."

"Check the nearest phone booth before you park. If she shows call me. I'll leave word with the answering service. If she should leave before I get there tail her and get in touch later.''

"Okay." Quinn rose. "That's all?"

The question made Fenner think. "Make a note of anyone else that goes in or out, other than couples who look as if they are tenants. Better grab a sandwich on your way. That may be all you'll get for dinner.''

When Quinn had left, Fenner snapped off his desk lamp, shrugged into his lightweight topcoat, and fixed the lock on the door before he went out. Alice Maxwell put down the paperback she had been reading and, despite the overtime, gave him her quick smile. A bubbly, competent twenty-two-year-old with a lovely complexion and pretty eyes, she was engaged to a young intern, and Fenner was increasingly happy to know it would be at least a year and a half before he had to look for another girl. Now she handed him the authorization Browning had signed and he said:

"Who was that other caller you tried to tell me about?"

"I don't know. Some hippie type.''

Fenner's eyes opened. "A hippie? Here? He or she?"

"At first I wasn't sure and then I noticed the curves. You could hardly help it. Tight denim pants, a black jacket, beads, long, lank-looking black hair."

"What did she want?"

"I don't know. She asked for you. When I said you were out and asked her name she asked when you'd be back. I said five — that's what you told me, isn't it? — and she said she'd wait. She sat down, but not very still. Chain-smoked, wiggled her foot — she had dirty sneakers on — and shortly after Mr. Browning came she said she couldn't wait any longer but would try to reach you later." She shrugged. "Never would tell me her name."

Fenner said okay, and thanked her for waiting. She stood up and examined her face in her vanity mirror. Apparently deciding it would do, she picked up her bag and reached for her coat. She was about to open the door when it swung to meet her and a man named Sam Carter came in. After he had watched her leave he turned to Fenner.

"I was in the neighborhood and took a chance you might still be in."

Fenner waited, searching for and finally finding a possible reason for the call. Carter was a friend of Kent Murcock's and a feature writer for the past couple of years on the *Courier,* mostly for the Sunday editions. When Fenner nodded but remained silent he said:

"I was wondering if you'd seen or heard from Carol Browning in the past week or so."

The question somehow came as no surprise and confirmed Fenner's tenuous reasoning. For Carter was also a friend of the woman and he now confirmed this.

"I mean," he said, "we've been fairly friendly, you know. Some lunches, an occasional dinner. She's letting me use the old shooting shack on the north shore of the Cape weekends to work on my book. I know you did some work for her and I thought—well, I haven't been able to reach her in ten days or more."

Fenner reached for a cigarette to buy time, lit it with some deliberation. It was not his practice to talk about a client or a job with anyone not connected with that job. He knew that Carter's concern was logical and legitimate and the truth was simple enough: he hadn't heard from Carol or seen her. But even as he accepted the minor coincidence of Carter being in the neighborhood and stopping by, the coincidence was compounded when the door opened again and Alan Hubbard walked in.

For Hubbard had been Carol Browning's first husband until she had gone to Reno about three years earlier. Now, having been prepared by Carter's request, Fenner was more or less ready to accept Hubbard's presence. Hubbard had been seeing his ex-wife recently in much the same way Carter had. The difference, in Fenner's opinion and from his observations, was that Hubbard was still in love with the woman and deeply concerned about what was happening to her.

Now he stopped short, the doorknob still in his hand. His glance moved from Fenner to Carter. Then, deciding to come in anyway, he spoke politely and with some embarrassment.

"Oh, sorry. I didn't mean to barge in.

Didn't think you'd even be here actually," he added to Fenner. "I'll wait outside if you'll be free before too long." Then, as an afterthought, "Hello, Sam."

"You're not interrupting anything," Carter said. "Join the huddle. I have an idea we're both here for the same reason."

"Are we?"

"I haven't been able to reach Carol for ten days or more. You too?"

"Well, yes. I've phoned several times. Tried the Brookline place too. Even drove down to the Cape to see if she was hiding in the old shooting lodge."

He hesitated, still showing some embarrassment, as though not sure quite how to go on. Finally he said:

"What happened is I ran into George Browning on the street a few minutes ago and stopped him. I asked if he knew where Carol was and he said not at the moment. I asked him what he meant by that and he said he knew where she'd been but not where she was. Then I said: 'Well, where was she?' and he said: 'Why don't you ask Jack Fenner?' "

Fenner had been thinking hard while the

two had been talking and his eyes and thoughts had been occupied by the difference in the two men who were concerned by Carol Browning's apparent disappearance.

Carter was a somewhat stocky man in his early thirties, with receding dark hair, amber eyes, and dark-rimmed glasses. In Fenner's opinion he looked more like a writer than a newspaper man, possibly because of the mustache and the mini-beard which was more than a goatee but less than full. His slacks and jacket were decently cut but rumpled-looking. He apparently had always worked for newspapers and had come here from the West Coast two or three years previously.

Alan Hubbard, on the other hand, had always been here in the sense that there had been Hubbards prominent as educators and bankers as long as anyone remembered. He was perhaps six-foot-one and a hundred and seventy-five, and had rowed bow on a very good Harvard crew. He had gone on to business school and had been married right after graduation. He had moved immediately into the family business, a smallish and conservative investment firm that specialized more in trusts and institutional accounts than day-to-day trading. A few years younger than Carter, his eyes were dark blue, his medium-blond hair conservatively cut, as was his dark-gray business suit. According to Fenner's information he was a bit shy with women, but if his manner was usually reserved it was always genuine . . .

"Sorry," Fenner said, snapping out of his mental speculations and aware that someone had asked a question.

"I asked," Hubbard said patiently, "what Browning meant by his statement that I ask you."

Fenner considered the question and decided that under the circumstances he could stretch his code of ethics. That this could have been prompted by his active dislike of Browning did not occur to him.

"George Browning hired me to do a job for him a few minutes ago. Ordinarily that would be nobody's business but ours. In this case he and you and I want the same thing."

"Which is?" Hubbard said politely.

"To find Mrs. Browning."

"Then she *is* missing," Carter said.

"Since when?" Hubbard asked.

"A couple of hours."

"From where?" Carter asked and Hubbard said: "Where was she?"

Fenner told them as briefly and as succinctly as he could and the reaction was as different as the two men, though the shock of Carol's commitment was the same. Carter's phrases were profane and explosive. Hubbard remained silent, but Fenner observed the tightening of the good-looking face and the hard glint in the eyes.

Before either could question him further, Fenner looked pointedly at his strap watch.

"I'm late for an appointment," he said. "There's nothing more I can tell you anyway."

"But you'll let us know?" Hubbard said stiffly.

"Browning's paying the freight. The odds are the police will pick her up first, but if I should happen to locate her before they do, my first obligation is to tell him. In either case I doubt if it will be too long before you get the word one way or another."

He opened the door and they got the message. Each in his own accents said thanks and he waited, the door still open, until he heard them enter the automatic elevator. Then, after another glance about, he turned off the lights and locked up.

4

Kent Murdock had a three-room apartment in an old, narrow-front brownstone that had been remodeled to make one apartment on each of the three upper floors. Jack Fenner had been there often and he visualized the layout as he climbed the flight of stairs to the second floor.

A large living room, comfortably furnished; good-sized bedroom with an oversized bed, a snug but adequate kitchen. There had once been a large dining alcove, but Murdock had partitioned it off to make a darkroom complete with sink, enlarger, and working counters as well as a file of negatives taken over the years that he felt worth keeping.

Murdock, jacket off but tie in place, opened the door almost immediately, waiting until Fenner preceded him. Still wondering about the urgency of his friend's call but more concerned about his recent visitors on the short ride over, he stepped past the little entryway, took one step, and then stopped in his tracks.

Jack Fenner seldom showed surprise. His background as a plainclothesman and later a detective had trained him well in his profession as an investigator, but this time the facade cracked. The brows snapped up as the agate eyes went wide, and for a long second his jaw hung slack.

She was sitting on the divan looking right at him, and the picture she presented was so incongruous here in his friend's apartment that he was momentarily baffled. His mind began racing before he could control his features, and as he thought: *What the hell would a hippie be doing here?* his brain whipped back to the description Alice Maxwell had given him about the unknown caller who had left his office before he returned.

Tight denim pants, a black jacket, open now to disclose a white jersey or T-shirt handsomely filled at the bustline; beads, lank black hair . . .

"Hello, Jack."

The voice helped; so did the smile. In another second he might have put it all together, but as he got his face in order and closed his mouth, she reached up and the black hair came off in one hand and he watched in wonderment as Carol Browning ran her fingers through the natural blond hair and fluffed up the back of the shoulder-length bob.

Fenner looked at Murdock and the grin that was there brought a touch of annoyance. Finally he backed to the nearest chair, sank into it, stretched out his legs, and crossed his ankles. He blew out his breath and motioned toward the tray on the coffee table.

"Okay, you've had your fun. Give me a drink, hunh?"

"Coming up," Murdock said and Fenner eyed the girl severely. "You were the hippie who came to my office."

"You weren't there."

"You could have waited."

"After George came storming in? I wasn't as confident of my disguise as you might think."

"So you came here?"

44

"I didn't have your home address and I remembered you had an unlisted number and" — she smiled at Murdock — "then I remembered that Kent loved me too, mostly because of my two brothers, I guess. So I phoned his office and he'd gone and I caught him here and asked if I could come."

Murdock handed Fenner a bourbon and water and the detective drank greedily. He watched his friend replenish the girl's glass and in that temporary silence his mind went back and he remembered things about the Grayson family — her maiden name — and the two brothers, now dead.

There were two Grayson brothers originally, Carol's father and an uncle, Lamont Grayson, who was at present the trustee of Carol's inheritance. Her grandfather had started the family business and when he died the lawyers decided the business was about equal in value to the more liquid investments in the estate. Lamont had taken the cash and bonds as his half and immediately departed for Europe and a life abroad. Carol's father had taken the business, which had gradually developed from small electric components to more sophisticated electronic devices, prospering nicely as the years went by.

The father had married a second time, to a widow with a son named Barry, older than Carol, and the boy had taken the Grayson name. When, a few years later, the second wife died, Grayson, the father, took over the job of educating the brood, but the death of the older son in Korea changed things. The second son had no great interest in the business, choosing teaching as his profession, so for tax as well as personal reasons the firm went public with the elder Grayson keeping a large block of stock.

Then, to compound the old man's grief, the second son had been killed in a traffic accident. By this time Carol's stepbrother had taken off for Switzerland to go to a hotel school and was living on an allowance.

Perhaps quite naturally, having no real mother since she was small, and being the youngest child and only girl, Carol was spoiled. She was still spoiled, selfish, and somewhat unpredictable when she married Alan Hubbard at eighteen. The old man lived long enough to see this, and when he died the estate was left in trust with Lamont Grayson, the prodigal brother now back from Europe and already handling some of his brother's affairs, named co-executor and trustee, a job he would hold until the fifteenth when the estate would revert to Carol . . .

The sound of voices finally penetrated Fenner's musings, and as his mind came back he picked up the conversation and heard Murdock saying something about wasn't it time Carol told them the whole story. To Fenner he said:

"You know where she's been the past couple of weeks?"

"Yes."

Murdock blinked his surprise. "You do? How?"

"Why do you think Browning came to my office?"

The girl's eyes widened and her mouth went round. "Oh . . . You mean he came—" She tried again. "He told you I'd been at Ufford?"

She stopped there as Fenner produced the authorization Browning had signed, and the check. She examined them, a growing whiteness at her cheekbones.

"Of course," she said. "I suppose I should have guessed. He hired you to find me?"

"Right. Hopefully before the police do."

"Oh, dear," she said, her despair showing and the hazel eyes full of trouble until she conquered the mood and stuck out her chin. "But surely you don't have to tell him. I mean, not yet."

That look, the tone of voice reminded Fenner of a word Frank Quinn had used in his description. Arrogant. *A little arrogant,* to be precise. And now he thought, yes. And why not, spoiled as she was, with money never a problem; a proper finishing school, an impeccable social background, and a year abroad before marriage?

Also beautiful, with smooth skin still slightly tanned from the recent summer sun. Slender, with a proper roundness that not only seemed shapely but firm. Tallish and proudly held, she had the speech and manner of expression that was an odd mixture of Back Bay and the tough, cynical vernacular of the day.

"Yeah, Jack," Murdock said. "What

about it? Would she have to go back?"

"I don't know the law on that."

"You studied it."

"In night school," Fenner said dryly. "No degree. I should think—" He stopped, brow wrinkling as some new thought came to him. He turned back to the girl. "George said he came by your place a couple of weeks ago and found you out of your skull, hallucinating, thinking you could fly. He said it was all he could do to keep you from jumping out the window. How about it?"

"He could be right. I do remember it was a feeling I'd never had before. I guess I had to be high."

"On what?"

"Who knows?"

"You didn't take anything?"

"Two drinks."

"Did George fix them?"

"Yes—come to think of it."

Fenner glanced at Murdock. "Acid? LSD?" When Murdock shrugged he continued to the girl: "Have you ever been on a trip?"

"Never."

"Pot?"

"Not more than three or four times."

"What's the next thing that happened?"

"I don't know, not really," she said, sounding as if she meant it. "I had the vague feeling I was seeing things I'd never experienced before. Actually the next thing I knew for sure was that I woke up in a strange bed in an unfamiliar place. They told me I was at Ufford."

"Do you trust this Dr. Garic?"

"I think so, yes."

"Have you seen him since?"

"He came to the hospital one day last week."

"How long had you been there then?"

"About a week, I guess. When I found out where I was I started yelling and they loaded me with tranquilizers. Later they cut them down to three a day. I was all right when I saw Garic."

"You gave him hell?"

"Of course I did. I asked him why I had been committed and he said I needed immediate hospitalization, and I said But why here? He said it was George's decision. As my husband he had the final say. He, Garic, wanted to send me back to

Connecticut where they had a history on me, but George insisted on Ufford. Some nonsense about the shock value of being there curing me once and for all. Apparently Garic had no choice."

"Did he describe your condition when he came to your apartment?"

She nodded, her manner strangely subdued. "I guess I was just the way George told you I was. I certainly must have taken some kind of drug."

"How long is the commitment?"

"Garic said thirty days."

Fenner looked at Murdock. "I suppose you could get a lawyer and Garic and petition the court." To the girl: "Your uncle's a lawyer, isn't he?"

"Lamont? Yes."

"How come you didn't phone him from Ufford?"

"I did, twice. He wasn't in."

"What about your ex? You're still good friends."

"Alan?" Her abrupt laugh was tinged with bitterness. "I was too ashamed."

"And Sam Carter? He's a friend too, isn't he? A newspaperman might help."

"I tried him over the past weekend and he must have been at the lodge on the Cape working on his book. Then when Monday came and they gave me a parole pass I decided to try it on my own."

"A parole pass means what?"

"I have the freedom of the grounds."

Fenner gestured with his empty glass and when Murdock started to make a refill he said:

"Did she tell you how she got this far?"

"No," Murdock said. "When she knew you were coming she said she wasn't going to tell it twice and I'd have to wait." He asked the girl if he could fix her drink and when she shook her head Fenner said:

"So you walked off, just like that? Did you have any money?"

"Not a dime. The nurses keep it."

"So you hitchhiked. On the Thruway?"

"On the old road behind the place. I was afraid I'd be picked up on the Thruway. I walked about a mile, I guess; it seemed like five."

And then Fenner was listening as she spoke of the truck driver who had given her a lift, and the wedding ring she had given him for a ten-dollar loan.

"A gold one?" Fenner asked.

"Platinum and diamonds." She grimaced. "I bought it myself."

Fenner went over to the stand near the bedroom door and picked up the directory and the telephone. It had an extra-long cord and he brought it back to the coffee table and took out a notebook and pencil.

"Bayside Trucking? And the guy's name was Megan?" He looked up a number, made a note, pushed the book toward Murdock. "See how many Megans there are."

When he got an answer at Bayside Trucking he asked for the night dispatcher, identified himself and his profession. He said he'd like to get in touch with a driver named Megan and could he have the man's home address.

"Sorry," the dispatcher said. "It's against company rules. You want Megan, you'll have to come to the office."

"I told you it was important," Fenner said. "You'd do him a favor if you could, wouldn't you?"

"Sure."

"Then take my name and this telephone number." He read it off. "Call Megan. Tell Megan I want him to call back. Tell him it's about a diamond-and-platinum wedding ring. Oh, yes. And tell him he might save himself a lot of grief if he calls back in the next fifteen minutes. Okay?"

Kent Murdock had been leaning back, his grin absent but admiring as he watched his friend work. They had known each other first back in the days when he was on the street with a camera and Fenner was a young precinct detective. They were both married at the time but they'd get together for a drink occasionally and there were times when he was able to give Fenner a possible lead, favors that were repaid when Fenner would tip off Murdock to some imminent arrest so that he could beat the opposition to the scene.

When Fenner eventually got fed up with the red tape and regulations that are a necessary part of a police officer's life, he went to work for a national agency, and for a time their paths had crossed less frequently. Later, when Fenner went in for himself, there had been occasions when

Murdock could use him — at the *Courier*'s expense — on certain assignments where professional help was needed.

They had, he decided long ago, much in common. Both were moderately tall, with Fenner just a little, maybe five pounds, the leaner, more angular of face. Both had dark hair, but while Fenner's was thinning, the widow's peaks more prominent, Murdock's was thicker and growing more noticeably grayer at the sides. There was, too, a common interest in photography, and Fenner was as good in his way as Murdock was in his; this, plus a closet full of electronic gear that he knew how to use, was one of the reasons Fenner was able to charge the fees he did.

Even back in the days when he was a cop, there was a little something that set him apart from his associates. To see him in plain clothes few would have suspected that he was a police detective. He didn't have flat feet. He was better dressed and better educated than most. He never was a muscleman, but he did have a fast pair of hands when the occasion demanded. Murdock had never seen him hit a man more than twice without dumping him, but when it came to breaking down a suspect he counted more on reason, logic, and common sense.

Only his eyes might have betrayed him to a trained psychologist. Seldom mean, they were quick and observant, with an ever-ready air of suspicion that was less a part of his character than the acquired trait of a man who had to deal for the most part with suspicious persons . . . Aware that Fenner had again turned to Carol, he continued to listen.

"So this Megan dropped you at the Square; then what?"

"I was still scared, petrified that someone would recognize me. The sight of a uniformed policeman horrified me. So I went to this hippy boutique I knew and traded my dress and shoes for this." She made a down-the-front sweep of one hand. "They wanted the whole ten but I held out for subway fare. I had to walk to your office."

The telephone rang to punctuate the sentence and Fenner winked and picked it up.

"Hello, Megan," he said to the voice that answered. "Jack Fenner." He gave his office address. "About that ring. You can bring it to my office any time tomorrow morning."

The reply was surly and defiant. "Why the hell should I?"

"I'll tell you. If you don't show I'll try your wife first and let her know you pick up dames when you're on the road. Your office will want to know you've been breaking regulations. That ring, incidentally, is the McCoy, which means it qualifies for grand theft if I have to get tough . . . Any time in the morning, Megan," he added when there was no immediate reply. "If I'm not there my secretary will hand you fifteen bucks, ten for the loan and five for cab fare. Make it easy on yourself, hunh?"

Carol's laugh bubbled as he hung up. "My, my, Jack," she said. "How you talk."

Fenner chuckled in spite of himself and Murdock said: "Okay, Jack, we've got the story. Now what? You can't turn her in tonight; not until we figure something out and she sees an attorney."

Fenner's frown bit deeper. "Yeah, but—"

"She paid you a lot of dough over the past months. You owe her something."

"Ethically—"

"To hell with that. You haven't cashed the check. Call Browning and tell him you've thought it over and changed your mind."

Fenner knew what he was going to do. He didn't like it but he liked the alternative less. For once he was going to compromise, though weasel was the word that came to him. He took a quick glance at the girl and the anxious, pleading look he saw in her eyes was too much for him.

"Well, she's got to have a place to stay," he said gruffly. "She can't go to a hotel in that outfit."

"We discussed that," Murdock said and then grinned openly. "I only have a double bed and Carol said no."

"I said no such thing," she said, trying to sound severe.

"Jack's got twin beds at his place. How about that?"

She pretended to consider the suggestion. She looked at Fenner and tried to suppress a smile. "I think not," she said finally using her aristocratic accents. "I know myself," she added, "but I'm not sure how well Jack resists temptation."

Fenner was reaching for the telephone as she finished and now he dialed Alice Maxwell's number. "Alice . . . Jack Fenner. Look, have you still got that convertible-couch thing in your living room? Could you put up a female guest for tonight? In case you're wondering, it's Mrs. George Browning."

As Fenner had expected, there was no hesitation. "Sure, Mr. Fenner. She can have the bedroom."

"I don't think she'd accept that, Alice. Just make that convertible into a bed. We'll probably be along in a half hour or so."

He glanced up, pleased, expecting at least a nod of approbation. Instead Carol was frowning at him.

"I have to have some clothes," she announced flatly, her tone suggesting there could be no argument.

"Where are you going to get them at this hour?" Murdock said, as surprised as Fenner.

"At my place. Jack can pack a bag for me."

"How do I get in?" Fenner said.

"I have a key." She produced it from a side pocket.

It took Fenner a few seconds to digest this because there was one point he couldn't understand. "I thought the nurses took everything but toilet articles."

"They do."

"Then how—"

"My place has the same superintendent as the apartment house next door. I went and asked him for a duplicate. I forgot the wig at first and I thought he was going to flip. I snatched it off. I told him I was going to a masquerade when he recognized me."

Fenner glanced at Murdock, who let his brows climb and shrugged silently. Fenner was still struggling with some mental chaos. When he could he said:

"You went there from Cambridge?"

"No, I came to your place first."

"Why take the chance and go to your place at all?"

"I needed cash. I was broke. I didn't know where you lived and I had one thin dime left. Luckily Kent was in. I asked him could I please come over and to please call you and ask you to come too — as soon as you could."

She would have said more but Fenner stopped her with an upraised palm while he tried to make some time sequence from the total confusion in his mind.

He had entered the office about 5:30 to find Browning waiting. They had talked, Murdock's phone call interrupting. He had glanced at his watch then to find it was 5:38. Browning had left by 5:45. Maybe three minutes with Frank Quinn and another five with Hubbard and Sam Carter . . .

"Then you didn't come here from my office?" When she shook her head, he regarded Murdock with narrowed eyes. "She wasn't here when you phoned?"

"No. She called me and I called you."

"When *did* she get here?"

"About ten minutes, maybe less, before you did. About twenty after six I guess."

Fenner tabulated this mentally and turned again to the girl. "You left my office before 5:30"

"Not much before."

"You then spent your last dime and called Kent. What did you do between, say, 5:30 or so and 6:20 when you got here?"

"Oh, for heaven's sake," she said as though the whole thing were much too simple to explain. "I told you. I had to have some money if only for cab fare. There was some at my place, so after I phoned I started walking. It must have been five miles—" She stopped, seeing Fenner's grin. "Well, a mile anyway," she added defiantly.

"Okay. So you got the key from the super and went up."

"Not then. I told you I was scared. I walked up one side of the street and down the other looking for George's car. I waited—I'm not sure how long—across the street getting up my nerve; then I marched across the street and walked in."

"This," Fenner said, holding up the key, "fits the downstairs door?"

"No."

"How come?"

She sighed audibly and gave him a look of patient suffering at such obtuseness.

"Because people kept forgetting their keys and going next door to the poor man at all hours to get him to let them in. He finally got fed up and sent us tenants a note. No more running back and forth unlocking doors. Leave it unlocked if we liked. He's a late-show TV addict and he usually comes by around one to lock up. By that time everyone—I'm the only single: by that I mean the others are older couples—are in."

"So you went up?"

"And into my bedroom and the bottom drawer of the bureau under some sweaters. I always keep some cash in the house—"

"How much?"

"For God's sake, Jack!" she snapped, no longer the aristocrat. "How the hell can that matter? I told you I was scared, you dum-dum!"

"I always ask a lot of questions," Fenner said good-naturedly.

"Several hundred, sometimes a thousand or two. So I grabbed some twenties and ran."

"How long would it take you to pack a bag?"

"Oh, come off it, Jack," Murdock cut in impatiently. "You're not questioning a suspect. Why should she press her luck? She told you she was scared."

"Petrified that George would walk in."

"Yeah," Fenner said, chagrined when he realized what he had been doing. "Sorry. It gets to be a habit, I guess."

But his mind was still busy as they accepted his apology. Trying to straighten out the time progression he found himself wondering if Frank Quinn had been parked there at the time. Finally admitting it didn't matter, he finished his drink and stood up.

"Let's go. You can wait while I go up and pack a bag and then I'll take you out to Alice's."

"Well," she said, "finally."

She took a deep breath, breasts thrusting at the thin white jersey. She gave him her best smile, a look of triumph in her eyes. She turned to Murdock when he rose with her, kissed him on the mouth in an affectionate, unaffected way.

"Thanks, Kent." She gave Fenner a sly, mischievous grin. "I like you much better than Jack."

5

Jack Fenner had driven about four blocks in the direction of Carol Browning's apartment when he changed his mind. Sensing the change, Carol asked him where he was going and he explained. There was, he said, no sense in leaving her alone in a car parked in front of her apartment while he went upstairs. The fact that probably no one would recognize her in her hippie get-up could, he said, work in reverse since curious cops might well stop to question a lone hippie parked in that area.

Now, having taken her to Alice Maxwell's modest three-room walk-up out beyond the medical school and explained the situation, he cruised slowly down the one-way street where Carol lived. There was a space directly in front of the door but he passed this up to take another opening near the corner. He walked back the fifty yards looking for Frank Quinn and finally spotted his car parked diagonally across from the entrance.

Fenner did not know the history of the four story brick-and-granite building where Carol had a third-floor apartment. It could have been a townhouse of some former tycoon, not a brownstone but built flush with the sidewalk, with a recessed entrance and a massive, forbidding, all-wood door. Whatever it had once been it now housed eight expensive and plush apartments, two to a floor.

On its right stood a squarish, seven-story apartment building, several steps down in class, and it was ironic that it was here that George Browning had his two-room efficiency used almost exclusively for entertaining certain girl friends, a fact Fenner had noted in previous reports to Carol. On the left was another four-story structure, a professional building used almost exclusively by doctors.

Now, stopping at the curb where Quinn could see him, Fenner held up one hand, making a circle of thumb and forefinger to indicate that all was well and to stay put.

The massive door was unlocked as Carol had predicted and he rode a small but silent elevator to the thrid floor, key in hand.

The apartment was in darkness as he stepped inside, but having been there before he was familiar with the switch on the inside casing. This left him in a square entryway with a coat closet on his right, and he kept moving, flicking another switch. There was no overhead light, but three strategically placed table lamps provided sufficient illumination.

He had gone down the two steps into the long, dropped living room, intent only on a bedroom beyond and his assignment, when he saw the body.

That stopped him while a barrage of conflicting thoughts and emotions assailed him. Moving nothing but his head, he let his breath out slowly and inspected the expensively furnished room with its wood-burning fireplace, the over-sized divan with its antique end tables, the rich Orientals, the built-in television. There was no sign of a struggle and everything seemed in place as he remembered it but the drawer of a small maple table that stood against the wall at his immediate left. This drawer had been pulled part way out.

When he was ready he moved, still a little shaky and edgy, breathing through his mouth, every sense alert. He could not yet see the face but, remembering the expensive slacks and jacket, he was convinced that this was George Browning.

He saw then that the man lay on his back, ankles oddly crossed in an attitude of complete relaxation he had noticed before in similar instances. One hand was folded naturally across the upper part of the chest, the other was upbent at the elbow, palm upward like a sleeping child.

By this time he had seen the two guns, but he continued to the body, in no hurry now since he knew the police had to be called, dropping to one knee beside it, seeing now the two small stained holes in the shirt front, one almost dead center and the other perhaps four inches to the left.

There was very little blood and he sensed that a small-caliber gun had done the damage. He put the back of his hand against a cheek gone dead white, not sure whether he detected some faint warmth.

Because he had seen medical examiners work too often not to know and understand some of their methods, he put a hand on either side of the face and tested the neck for stiffness. When he had tried to flex one knee he made his own guess. An hour at least —

A glance at his watch told him it was 7:40 and he recalled that it had been roughly 5:45 when he had seen Browning last. He did not know just when he had left Murdock's or how long it had taken him to drive Carol to Alice Maxwell's apartment and return here but Browning had been alive two hours ago and he was now dead.

The gun closest to the upflung hand was a .38 S. & W. with a two-inch barrel, and by moving to the proper angle he could tell one shot had been fired.

The other, closer to the feet, was a .22. In most homicides these days when a .22 was used it was usually some cheap automatic of foreign make, often obtained through the mails. Saturday Night Specials was the term sometimes given them. This, on the other hand, was a small, short-barreled revolver, a model he had seldom seen.

On his feet once more and remembering what he had to do, he tried not to think about Carol Browning and the timetable he had fashioned in his mind earlier. She admitted having come here; the question he could not ignore was, When?

He walked away from the body, traces of shock lingering, not at the fact of murder or the victim but the time and place of his discovery. Having seen death in most of its violent forms, he had learned not to waste his capacity for sympathy and understanding on something he could do nothing about. Only one thing was always the same: the futility of the act, the tragedy for everyone concerned no matter how innocent. George Browning was, for whatever reason, a victim no better or worse than others who had preceded him throughout history and still others who would follow.

Although he had been in this apartment twice for a drink, he had not seen the rest of it, and now he went exploring, turning lights on and off in three bedrooms, one quite small and possibly designed for a maid. There were three baths, though the small room had only a stall shower. What he considered bedroom number two looked long unoccupied, and after flipping the light switch he concentrated on Carol's room.

Sizable, with two windows, it had an oversized bed with a lacy counterpane. There was a vanity apparently fashioned from some antique piece Fenner could not identify, a long maple bureau with an antique-framed mirror; a chaise upholstered in a patterned print that could have been satin. After his first glance he stepped to the sliding-door closets that occupied most of one wall.

He had never seen so many clothes in his life; the same held true for the racked shoes. The darker corner of the right-hand side was stacked with luggage and it took him a moment to decide whether to make a selection from a matching set complete with hatbox in a medium blue, or the equally complete set done in rawhide. Selecting a twenty-inch case in blue as being less conspicuous he tossed it on the bed and opened it.

The selection was so vast it confused him and he had to concentrate. In the end he took one simple tailored dress in navy. He found a pair of navy shoes to match; then, moving to the bureau, he selected a cardigan, went back and got an odd woolen skirt and a pair of spectators. From the drawer above he found two bras, a slip, a girdle, a pair of stockings, a pair of pantyhose, a nightgown (low-necked the way he liked them), slippers, a filmy robe and, as an afterthought, a white blouse.

Since there was a little room left he selected a silver-backed brush and comb from the vanity, took a lipstick at random. From the bathroom he took a toothbrush, paste; a small leather case that looked like a manicure set became the last item.

At the door to the outer hall he fixed the lock so he could get in without a key, an instinctive gesture he did not attempt to analyze. Out on the street he walked quickly to his car and locked the case in the trunk. Once again in front of the building he made another gesture to the shadowy Quinn, who, mistaking the signal, started to open the door until he interpreted the gesture correctly and resumed his seat.

Back upstairs, Fenner paid no further

attention to the still figure on the floor but went to the telephone, picked it up, thought, replaced it. The routine was to call the precinct but since homicide would be brought in shortly he decided to call direct, hoping for Lieutenant Bacon, a long-time acquaintance of his and a friend of Kent Murdock's.

He got homicide at once, but here his luck deserted him. Bacon, he was told when he identified himself, was in Vermont.

"In October?" Fenner said. "What the hell for?"

"Foliage."

"Yeah," said Fenner, admitting that there was no prettier country when the fall foliage was turning. He hesitated then, knowing a Captain Lane headed the department. The trouble was that he had no liking for the veteran captain, a feeling that was mutual and of long standing. That left him one man for whom he had some respect. Joe Gaynor.

"How about Sergeant Gaynor?"

"Hang on."

"Joe," he said a moment later. "Jack Fenner."

"Hi, Jack," Gaynor said. "How you doin' these days?"

"Okay. Listen, I've got a little job for you."

"Like what?"

"A brand-new homicide."

There was a pause and Gaynor's tone grew wary. "Where are you?"

"On the scene," Fenner said and gave the address. "Third floor. The street door is unlocked."

"You call the precinct?"

"No."

"Why not, you know the drill?"

"I wanted to get Lieutenant Bacon but they tell me he's in Vermont. Captain Lane I can do without."

"Lane you'll probably get before we're through but I'll be right over. Stay put, Jack, and don't snoop."

Fenner hung up, glanced about, and selected a Boston rocker well away from the body and close to the entrance. He got a cigarette going, slumping a bit as he set the rocker in motion, his mind busy. Then the buzzer sounded, a loud and startling noise in the otherwise quiet room.

He checked his rocking and leaned forward, elbows on the chair arms, his eyes narrowed and intent. He listened to a second buzz and started to get up, not wanting to let the caller get away; then he heard someone try the knob. When the door opened he came to his feet expectantly as a man appeared at the top of the two steps leading to the room, a florid-faced, elegantly tailored man with a mustache and thick gray hair showing beneath the dark-gray homburg.

This, Fenner knew, was Lamont Grayson, Carol Browning's uncle, and he stayed very still as the other came down the steps and then stopped abruptly, almost in recoil, as he spotted the body.

Rooted there, his jaw sagged as his eyes went wide and he said: "George!" his voice tentative and uncertain. "George?" he called once more. Then, some instinctive message warning him that he was not alone, his glance darted sideways and he saw Fenner.

"Is that George Browning?" he said, no recognition in his gaze. "What happened to him?"

"Somebody shot him with that little .22 on the floor."

"Shot? Good God, is he dead?" The florid face was suddenly grim, the voice severe. "Who are you? Do I know you?"

"We've met. Jack Fenner. I'm a private investigator."

"Fenner?" He worked the word over. "Fenner? Oh, yes, I remember. And could I ask what you're doing here?"

"I was looking for Mrs. Browning," Fenner said and then a new and sudden idea came to him and he cursed himself for not thinking of it before. Ignoring Grayson, he stepped to the telephone and dialed Kent Murdock's number. "Kent? I'm glad I caught you."

"I was just going out for some dinner."

"Maybe you'll want to hold it up."

"Trouble? Did you get the bag?"

Fenner, ignoring the question, said: "I know you spend most of your time these days sitting on your duff in that little office of yours, but I thought you might want to come over to Carol Browning's apartment."

"Oh? Why?"

"Somebody shot Browning twice in the

chest. He was on the floor when I walked in."

There was a brief pause before Murdock said, drawing the word out: *"J-e-s-u-s!* Did you get Carol to your girl's place?"

"Yep."

"What about the clothes?"

"Taken care of."

"Call the law?"

"Sure."

"Who?"

"I tried for Bacon and drew Joe Gaynor; they should be here."

"If you called headquarters our man in the pressroom will get someone over there, but I'll be along."

"They probably won't let you up," Fenner said, "but hang around and we'll talk."

He cradled the telephone to find Grayson watching him intently. Now he spoke slowly, his tone suspicious.

"May I ask *why* you were looking for Mrs. Browning?"

"Her husband hired me to find her."

"Hired you? When?"

"Around five thirty, quarter of six. How

about you, Mr. Grayson? Were you looking for her?"

"I certainly was."

"Why?"

"Because I haven't been able to reach her. I was away for the weekend and since then I've called at least twice a day. I was afraid something was wrong."

"You have a key?"

"Certainly not. If I hadn't been able to get in I'd have got the superintendent next door. But if he" —he gestured toward the figure on the floor— "hired you to find her she must have been missing. For how long?"

"Since sometime before four this afternoon."

"Nonsense," Grayson said irritably. "A husband doesn't hire a private detective to find a wife that's only been missing a couple of hours. Where is she supposed to be missing from?"

"The State Hospital at Ufford."

The statement shook the other man. Once again his jaw sagged before he could control it. He seemed to be having difficulty assimilating the thought.

"I don't believe it," he said finally,

dismissing the idea as preposterous. "Who sent her there?"

"George did. Two weeks or so ago. He and a doctor named Garic committed her."

For some seconds Grayson seemed on the verge of further argument, but something in Fenner's voice and manner must have convinced him because he glanced about, found an easy chair, and dropped heavily into it. As he did so the buzzer sounded again and Fenner, relieved that the law had finally arrived, went up the two steps and on through the vestibule.

6

Sergeant Joe Gaynor was a stocky aggressive man in his late thirties, a competent, by-the-book detective Fenner had known for some years. He also recognized, but did not know well, Gaynor's partner, a taller, leaner, younger man who had sharp dark eyes and a quiet manner, and whose name was Reilly.

"Okay, Jack." Gaynor, coming into the living room and glancing suspiciously at Grayson after his first quick inspection of the body, turned to Fenner. "Fill me in. Has the guy on the floor got a name?"

"George Browning."

"His apartment?"

"His wife's," Fenner said, and went on to give the essentials while Reilly made some brief notes. When he finished, Gaynor, still regarding Grayson, said:

"What else did you touch beside the telephone?"

"Him"—Fenner nodded at the body—"to see if he was dead, and a few doorknobs."

"Why?"

"You walk in on a dead man, you like to be sure there's no one in the place, don't you?"

Gaynor grinned and said: "Correct. What time?"

"Maybe five minutes before I phoned headquarters."

Gaynor nodded and gestured to Reilly, who got the message and went to the telephone to put additional offical wheels in motion.

Gaynor said: "Who's this?"

"Mr. Lamont Grayson, Mrs. Browning's uncle . . . This is Sergeant Gaynor, Mr. Grayson."

"You arrived *after* Mr. Fenner?"

Grayson nodded, face still grim and the mustache flat above the tight, set mouth. "I did."

"Why?"

"I was looking for my niece. I hadn't

been able to reach her."

"And you, Jack? Or was this just a social call on the lady?"

Fenner knew what was coming. He'd gone through the routine himself in the past and he wanted to save his breath.

"Will Captain Lane be here?"

"Any minute."

"Why not let him carry the ball; then I'll only have to go over it once."

Gaynor thought it over, shrugged, and went to join Reilly at the body. Reilly had already run a pencil through the trigger guard of the heavier gun and as he placed it on a table Gaynor did the same with the .22.

"Touch them, did you?" he said to Fenner.

"You know better than that."

"Haven't had a makable print from a gun in years that I can remember, but you always have to try. The .38 was fired once apparently, the .22 twice. You figure the .22 did the job?"

"Looked that way to me."

Gaynor turned to Reilly. "Take a look around, Johnny. That heavy slug is either in this room or in the guy's body that used the .22 . . ."

The rest of the troops came in shortly, led by Captain Lane and followed closely by the photographer with his bulky case, the fingerprint expert, and soon after by an assistant medical examiner. When Lane had called the roll, he gave Fenner a flat, unfriendly stare, examined Grayson with some interest, but continued to Gaynor without speaking.

Fenner chose a chair off to one side where he could watch Grayson from an angle without being observed but the older man sat unmoving, distance in his fixed gaze. When the police continued their huddle, he let his thoughts drift back to things he had heard about the man and other things Carol Browning had paid him to find out.

He wasn't too familiar with Grayson's past beyond the fact that he had a law degree and had taken his inheritance in cash and fled to Europe. He had remained there for many years, mostly in France, where he had met and married a well-bred Frenchwoman many years earlier. Fenner wasn't sure what brought him home but assumed it to be a pressing lack of funds. At that time, his brother, Carol's father, had taken him into the firm as general counsel and it had been Lamont who had set up the stock offering when the company went public.

The childless marriage had lasted until Grayson, on a trip to Nevada while Carol was waiting out her residence, met and became infatuated with a busty blonde thirty years his junior. Fenner had checked her out too in his assignment for Carol, and learned that she had been the girl friend of some Mafia lesser-light until he drew five-to-ten for assault with a dangerous weapon. She had been dealing blackjack in Las Vegas at the time Grayson met her and Fenner wasn't sure whether he brought her back with him or whether she followed him. In any case, the liaison had continued since, its base a rather plush apartment that Grayson maintained for her.

When she was sure of the arrangement, his wife, being a Catholic and unwilling to divorce him, was able to extract a healthy monthly payment and now raised boxers in Vermont and was a part owner of a ski resort. Since then, Grayson and girl friend — her name was Mona Vail — were seen more frequently together at the better restaurants and the first nights of New York-bound shows here for a try-out . . .

Aware suddenly of some movement at one side, he glanced up to find Captain Lane staring down at him, topcoat spread by the hands-on-hip stance, the stub of an unlit cigar in his mouth. A loud, bluff man with a boxlike jaw and a blunt manner, he was jealous of his authority, a factor in the mutual dislike between him and Fenner that had started some years ago when Fenner was still on the city payroll. Now he said:

"You were here first, Fenner? You found him?"

"Right."

"How'd you get in?"

"The door was on latch," Fenner said, almost feeling the key in his pants pocket. "You can ask Mr. Grayson."

"Why? You could have fixed the lock after you got in. But skip that now. What brought you here?"

"I was looking for Mrs. Browning."

"Oh?" Lane rocked on heel and toe.

"Business or personal?"

"Business."

"Then you were working for somebody? Who?"

"Him."

Lane followed Fenner's glance to where the medical examiner was completing his examination of the body.

"You're saying Browning hired you to find his wife. Did you?"

"No," Fenner said, grasping the technicality that instead of finding Carol, he had been summoned to meet her.

"You got anything that says Browning hired you?"

Again Fenner reached into his pocket and produced the check and letter. He watched the cigar stub shift in the wide mouth as Lane examined them, noticed the head cock slightly before the captain returned them.

"Tough," Lane said. "Check isn't worth much now, is it?"

"That depends," Fenner said, trying to hold his annoyance in check, "on what Browning had for a will, if any. There has to be an executor, or administrator. I think he'll pay me whatever I earn."

"Pay you for what? You don't have a client any more."

"I think I do. It doesn't look good, an investigator having a client knocked off. There's sort of an obligation to help find out who did it."

"That's a lot of crap and you know it."

"Not to me, it isn't."

Lane studied him with flat, contemptuous eyes, shrugged, and dismissed him. "We don't mind a little help if you stay in line and keep out of our way . . . Now Mr. Grayson, Sergeant Gaynor tells me Mrs. Browning is your niece. You came here looking for her? How long had she been missing?"

"Mr. Fenner tells me that her husband had her committed to the State Hospital at Ufford some time ago," Grayson said stiffly. "I'm not sure when or why. I had no prior knowledge of this. I didn't try to get in touch with her until two or three days ago. I'd been out of town the previous weekend."

Lane turned back to Fenner. There had been little change in his expression, but the shrewd eyes had been busy as he listened to

87

Grayson and what he had just heard seemed to please him.

"Ufford, hunh?" he said. "Well, what do you know? Did Browning tell you why he had the lady committed?"

"I can only tell you what he told me," Fenner said and repeated the facts.

"Did he say how long *he* thought she'd been missing? He must have been kind of worried to pay your prices. Did he make a report to Missing Persons?"

Fenner knew some such question would be coming shortly and he had already made up his mind. Other authorities had already been notified of Carol's absence from Ufford; now with the city force looking for her for another reason the news would get out within hours if not before.

"She's been missing since sometime before four this afternoon," he said flatly, not looking at Lane now but watching Reilly working on the plastered wall, to one side of the little table by the vestibule and about chest-high.

By the looks of things he was fairly deep with his knife, cutting at the lath now and finally turning with something between

88

thumb and forefinger that Fenner knew must be the slug from the .38.

He snapped his thoughts back in time to hear Lane say, "Ufford" again, as though the word intrigued him in a self-satisified sort of way.

"Well, well," he said finally, eyes open now and new interest showing. "The lady walked away, the hospital people notified her husband, and he came to you. But he couldn't be bothered to tell the police, hunh?"

"He probably figured you'd get the word anyway."

Lane noticed that the medical examiner was on his feet and slipping into his coat.

"What do you say, Doc?"

"As a guess between one and two hours. If your photographer is finished, I'll send the boys up for him."

"You're right about the two hours," Fenner said. "He left my office around 5:45."

"Will you be able to make it closer after the P.M.?" Lane asked the doctor.

"I doubt it."

Lane nodded, teetered again and

regarded Fenner. "Where were you during the last two hours? Just for the record."

"I spent most of the time after I closed the office at Kent Murdock's place."

"Why?"

"Because he's an old friend of the lady. I thought he might have some ideas; it was possible she might even have got in touch with him."

"Did she?"

"Not that I know of," Fenner said, a little surprised at how easy the lie came.

"And you, Mr. Grayson, how do you account for your last couple of hours."

"I'm not sure I like your inference."

"No inference," Lane said blandly. "It's a question we always ask those who are close to the victim."

"I left my office shortly before five. Since then, until a short time ago, I was with someone."

Lane waited until he was sure Grayson had no intention of continuing before he said: "But you're not saying who?"

"Not at this time."

"What is your business, Mr. Grayson?"

Grayson unbuttoned the jacket of his

double-breasted blue suit, reached into a vest pocket, found a card case, and drew one, offering it between his first and middle fingers.

"An attorney, hunh?"

"Exactly." Grayson put his card case away. "And my advice to you, captain, would be to keep your questions in line."

"I don't think there's any need for more questions, counselor," Lane said smugly. "Find the dame and we wrap it up."

Grayson was shocked. "I don't believe it," he said and Fenner added: "Figure it."

"For you I shouldn't have to. When a husband is killed, who's the first suspect?"

"Okay, the wife."

"This one had obviously had trouble with the guy. The facts show she could have been off her rocker. She comes here, knowing there's this little .22 here, and he walks in on her . . . Sergeant!"

Gaynor turned from the photographer, who was packing his case. At the same time the door opened and two ambulance attendants entered with a basket stretcher and covered the body. Right behind came a uniformed precinct captain and two of his plainclothesmen. Fenner stopped looking as Lane spoke.

"Did you get the other slug? What kind of shape is it in?"

Gaynor held up the slug and Fenner could see it was a steel-jacket bullet with hardly any distortion.

"She holds the .22 on the husband," Lane continued to Grayson. "He knows he's going to get it and tries to get a shot off first —"

"If he was carrying a gun," Fenner cut in softly.

"— and either fires wild," Lane added, ignoring the comment, "or she opens up and the impact spoils his aim. Two guns like that. How else you going to figure it?"

"She had no motive," Grayson replied heatedly. "None whatsoever. She will come into a sizable inheritance next week. I happen to know Mr. Fenner did considerable work for her during the past months —"

"Yeah?" Lane interrupted. "What kind of work, Fenner?"

Fenner's grin was thin and humorless. "Confidential work, captain."

"Balls. Don't give me that."

"I know what I'm talking about," Grayson said. "She discussed the matter with me. She had more than enough evidence for an uncontested action for divorce." He rose abruptly. "I think I've had quite enough of this. I have an appointment."

He buttoned his jacket, buttoned the topcoat, adjusted the homburg. As he strode stiff-backed toward the two steps Lane called after him:

"Okay for now, counselor. But we'll probably ask you to stop by Headquarters in the morning and make a formal statement . . . Same for you, Fenner. Just a word of advice before you take off. You find the dame before we do, you get in touch. We'd hate to tag you with an accessory rap."

Fenner's angular face still held the same tight grin. He could have let it go at that but, in his dislike for Lane, he could not resist a final jab.

"You know the law about accessories as well as I do. You find Mrs. Browning, get her indicted, try and convict her; then I'm an accessory if I hold out. No indictment, no guilty verdict, no accessory charge."

He stood up to button his coat, seeing the pinkness growing in Lane's neck as he controlled his mounting irritation. He rammed a stiff forefinger against Fenner's chest once for emphasis.

"Okay, have it your way, Fenner. They tell me you used to be a good cop. You're a private now and I hear you're still doing pretty good. You want to keep it that way, watch your step. Oh, one thing more, the press will be laying for you outside. You clam up, understand? Any statement, I'll make it. You can tell 'em I said so!"

7

Captain Lane had been right about the press. They closed in on Fenner, six or seven of them, three with cameras. He knew most of them and he good-naturedly started edging his way through them saying: "Sorry, fellas, No comment . . . No comment."

"Come on," they said. "Give us a break . . . Nuts to that no-comment jazz . . . How did Browning get killed?"

There was more of the same, but Fenner's eyes were busy as he glanced between and above heads until he located Frank Quinn's car. At one side and taking no part in the huddle stood Murdock and with him was Sam Carter.

"Sorry," he said again. "The captain's orders were to clam up with you guys. If you cameras got a shot of the stretcher coming out you can blow; that's all you get

95

unless you want a shot of Lane." When the reporters said: "What about us?" he said: "All I can tell you is that George Browning was found shot to death in his wife's apartment. If you want to, you can say a local private investigator discovered the body."

He was clear of them then, hesitating on the curb to light a cigarette and nod to Murdock. Then he was moving across the street, not directly at Quinn's car but walking along the line of parked cars opposite until he reached it.

"My God!" Quinn said. "What the hell happened, Jack? I never saw so much law."

Murdock and Carter joined them and Fenner said: "Who tipped you off, Sam?"

"Our headquarters man phoned in the squeal and I happened to be in. Is the scoop right that somebody shot Browning?"

Fenner considered the question and the man. Murdock was entitled to know what happened and there were important questions to ask Frank Quinn.

"To you I'll talk," he said to Murdock, "but what about Sam? He's a reporter. A lot of this is confidential as hell or my ass could be in a sling."

"What about Sam?" Murdock demanded. "He's the best crime man on the staff. The syndicate series he's doing is even drawing threats. I saw one, a rewrite man overheard another that came over the phone. Also, he's a friend of Carol's. Maybe he can help."

Fenner considered the reporter, noting again the mustache and mini-beard. There was, in the files he had gathered for Carol Browning, a partial dossier on the man but nothing that might influence him in this case.

"All right, Sam. But this is strictly off the record. Agreed?"

"Agreed."

"Because if you leak anything I'll break your arm."

He told them then what he had found, omitting only the part about packing Carol's bag. He recited a resume of some of the conversations and what had transpired before he left. He was explaining about the two guns when a muffled curse from Carter stopped him.

Apparently the others heard it because there was a long moment of silence while they peered at Carter's bespectacled face. Fenner, seeing the consternation there, spoke first.

"What was that, Sam?"

"Those guns. You said one was a .22?"

"So?"

"That was the murder weapon?"

"Right."

"Revolver or automatic?"

"Revolver."

"Eight-shot?"

"I didn't count the chambers."

Carter blew his breath out in a loud and violent way. He cursed once more and then, seeming to get hold of himself, said:

"You talk about your ass being in a sling. *I think that was my gun.*"

After another long second of silence while the others tried to assimilate the statement Murdock said: "Your gun? How the hell did it get there?"

"It was already there," Carter said wearily. "I've had a gun for some time, a .32. I bought this little job six weeks or so ago when I started digging up facts for this crime series. Hell, it's even registered on my permit. I brought it up from the Cape. Browning used to slap Carol around pretty regularly. When he found out she was getting a file on him he started making threats. She was scared. I mean, really scared. I once saw her get almost hysterical about it because he'd tried to break the door in. So I gave her the gun and told her to use it if she had to. She was going to keep it in her bedroom, but I told her to have it handy by the entrance of the apartment. I said the idea wasn't to shoot anybody, but if her husband tried breaking in the door again a couple of shots in the floor would stop him. Christ, do you think he could have walked in on her and she used it?"

No one seemed to like the idea and Fenner realized that Carter knew nothing except that Carol had walked away from Ufford late that afternoon. It was not his intention to enlighten him, but there was a chance that Frank Quinn could help straighten some things out.

Now, having had no answer to his question, Carter said: "Has anybody seen her since? She wouldn't have much money, would she? Where could she go? . . . And look, you guys. The cops are going to trace that gun to me. I'll have to say what I did with it. Not only that, but Carol, when they find her, has got to back up my story. Oh, brother," he said and exhaled again. "Sam, boy, you're in a box . . . I have to tell the cops I gave it to her, don't I?" he added in a tone of supplication.

"Relax," Murdock said. "Tell 'em the truth."

"Frank" — Fenner turned to Quinn — "it's your turn . . . You both know Frank Quinn. He's had the place staked out the past couple of hours. When did you get here?"

"Well, I stopped for a take-out sandwich as you suggested. It's not much more than five minutes from our place to here; maybe five more waiting for the sandwich. I guess it was around five after six."

"Did you see Browning come?"

"Yeah, right after I got here."

"Who else?"

"Well, not counting two or three couples who looked as if they lived there — one came in, two came out — there was some guy in a Caddy convertible."

"You didn't recognize him?"

Quinn thought a moment, his glance moving from Fenner to Carter. "I'm pretty sure not," he said finally.

"Describe him."

"Good-sized, medium-young I thought. Bareheaded, plenty of hair but not shaggy. No topcoat, dark slacks, a lighter sports coat; could have been a medium gray or brown."

"Did you take down the license number?"

"Yeah, but I don't know if it will do you any good. It was from Colorado."

Fenner considered the statement, some latent bit of knowledge lurking far back in his brain that continued to escape him. There was, he knew, some connection between Colorado and Carol Browning, but what the hell was it? He looked to Murdock for help.

"Who did Carol know in Colorado? . . . Wait a minute!" He snapped his fingers. "She had a stepbrother."

"Right," Murdock said. "Mother married Carol's old man; took the name of Grayson, but I can't think of his first name."

"I've got it," Fenner said, real pleased

with himself. "This guy came back from Europe or someplace a year or so ago. I think Carol said he bought into a restaurant-bar in or around Denver. He's due to cut in for twenty percent of the estate under the old man's will."

"Next week," Murdock said. "The fifteenth."

Sure, Fenner thought. "Must've come east early," he said. "Probably been wondering where his stepsister is . . . What time was that, Frank?"

"I'd say around quarter of seven, give or take a couple of minutes."

"How long was he up there?"

"As a guess, five minutes."

"Long enough," Murdock speculated.

"Motive?" Carter said.

"None," Fenner said, "unless there was something between the two of them we don't know about . . . Who else, Frank?"

"Her ex-husband."

Murdock whistled softly. "No love lost there."

"Alan Hubbard," Fenner said, half-aloud, remembering Hubbard's recent call to his office. And Murdock was right about the bad feeling between the two. "What time?"

"Maybe seven o'clock."

"For how long?"

"About like the other guy."

"Who else?"

"You," Quinn said.

Fenner opened his mouth, ready to interrupt should Quinn try to mention the fact that he had come out with a packed suitcase and put it in the back of his car. But Quinn knew when to be quiet even though he could not understand the reasons for such tact. Instead he said, deliberately avoiding Fenner's gaze:

"Not too long after that, Lamont Grayson went in."

Again there were some moments of silence; then Fenner asked if there had been anyone else. Quinn seemed to be thinking. He was looking at Sam Carter, but his eyes were remote and full of thought.

"Well," he said finally, "There *was* this hippie."

Fenner looked at Murdock and their eyes locked while unpleasant things happened inside him. He looked pointedly at Sam

Carter, hoping Murdock would get the message. Heretofore he had given the reporter certain facts in confidence, but even to hint that this hippie was in fact Carol Browning would disclose their common knowledge that they had seen her and probably knew where she was. This, he decided, was none of Carter's business even with his pledge of silence. Under the circumstances he already knew enough. He proceeded warily, unwilling to go too far until he had Quinn alone.

"Hippie?" he said. "What hippie?"

"How do I know?"

"He or she?"

"At first I didn't know. Who can tell when they have that long hair? Then I decided it was probably a girl. I mean, she had some curves here and there."

"You saw her go in or out?"

"She didn't go in while I was here. I'm not absolutely sure she came out but—"

"Come on, Frank," Fenner said impatiently. "You saw this hippie. What was she doing?"

"Standing on the sidewalk. The building is built to the edge. I hadn't noticed any movement—you just can't keep staring at one spot hour after hour. I was lighting a cigarette. When I flipped the match out the window I spotted her. I figured she'd just stepped from that recessed doorway. What the hell, Jack, I'm interested in a tall blond broad with a yummy figure. I can't even tell you for sure what time it was. I didn't think it mattered."

Fenner nodded and decided to try one more question. "Would you say you saw this character before or after Browning had gone up?"

"To tell the truth I paid damn little attention to her but I'd say *after*. I wouldn't swear to it, understand, but that's the way I seem to remember it."

Again the vague timetable was churning round in Fenner's mind. Carol had admitted coming here. She had gone up, got some cash and, according to her, ran. Could it be possible that Browning had walked in on her, or that she had walked in on him? She had the little .22 and knew where it was. Under the pressure of panic, hysteria, or some physical threat from Browning—and he was quite capable of such an act—she could have used that gun. If she had the money she would most certainly drop the gun and run. If not would she shoot and still take time to grab the cash? Who could say what any individual would do under such circumstances?

Realizing such speculation was pointless and futile, he closed his mind to it. Once he had paper and pencil and had worked out a more accurate schedule he could try again. The important thing now was to get rid of Carter, to hold Murdock up until he could consult him, to have a few words with Quinn in private.

"Okay, Frank, stick around a minute, will you?" he said and took Murdock by the arm, guiding him to one side. "Where's your car?"

"Down by the corner," Murdock said, pointing.

"Mine's just across the intersection," Carter said.

Fenner, still holding Murdock's arm, pulled him to a stop. He said that since Murdock hadn't eaten why didn't they get a bite together. To Carter he said, hoping the reporter would get the implication of dismissal:

"Just remember, Sam. What you heard was strictly confidential."

"You told me," Carter said. "And so stop worrying, okay? You going to stop by the office, Kent?"

"Maybe later."

"Okay." Carter gave them a small salute. "See you."

Fenner stood where he was until Carter was some distance away. "Let me talk to Frank a minute. I want to get that bag to Carol; I also want to have a little talk with her. You want to come?"

"You know I do."

"We'll take my wagon since I've got the bag. We'll get a couple of quick martinis and maybe a hot sandwich." He let go of Murdock's arm and continued on to Quinn's car.

"Have you thought any more about that hippie, Frank? Can you pin the time down a little better?"

"Not yet. Maybe later when I'm alone and can reconstruct my impressions something may come. But what gets me is why the hell this hippie is so important? You asked if she came out — if she actually did come out — after Browning went up. This gives me an idea that maybe you think this hippie is a possible suspect."

Fenner, having nearly made up his mind, hesitated but a second or two. He had no reason, judging from past experience, not to trust Quinn. He would have no reason to break a confidence and as an attorney, he might, if cornered, be able to plead privilege. There could very well be a need for a man's continued help in working this out and it seemed better that he know the truth.

"I'll lay it out for you, Frank," he said. "Between you and me and Murdock. We're the only ones who know. That hippie happened to be Carol Browning!"

Even in the semi-darkness Fenner could see Quinn's mouth open part way and then shut. His shadowed eyes seemed to bulge a little. Finally, on a note of exhalation, he said: "Wow!" Then, suspiciously: "You've got to be kidding. Where would she get an outfit like that? Why?"

Aware that Quinn knew nothing of the

background Fenner filled him in, his voice clipped and intent as he recited the essentials. When he finished, Quinn blew out his breath again and shook his head, his admiration showing.

"What a doll! Imagine walking off and hitchhiking and trading a ring for a ten-dollar loan, and then being smart enough to get a hippie disguise good enough to fool her husband. And right there in your office, too. Where'd you take her, not to a hotel?"

"She's out at Alice's place for the night."

"Oh-ho!" Quinn said abruptly, like a man on the verge of some great discovery. "So that's why you came out to your car with that suitcase. You went in for some clothes. And Browning was already dead. How about that? You sort of took a chance, didn't you?"

"I didn't think so. All I did was hold up the police call five minutes. So now you know why what you saw is important. I'll have to tell Sergeant Gaynor you were working for me and you can take it from there. Tell him what you saw and when. That's why I want you to do some real thinking about our hippie friend."

"I could twist the time a bit."

"I wouldn't until you check with me. Keep vague with the sergeant." He gave him a friendly poke on the shoulder. "Just like you've been with me."

Quinn stepped on the starter. "I'll get it straightened out in my mind, Jack," he promised. "I'll do some thinking tonight when I get home. Maybe a couple of drinks will help."

Fenner found Murdock waiting quietly in his car and asked where he wanted to have the drinks and sandwich. Murdock said how about Gallager's, adding that they had marvelous beef sandwiches, either corned or roast.

8

To save time they ordered double martinis-with-twists instead of two singles. When they'd had their first grateful swallows, Fenner brought out his notebook and a pen, saying he had to get some kind of a timetable down on paper.

"Here, you write it down. If I talk it out maybe it will clarify things a little . . . You know," he added, "this will be a tight schedule. Quinn and I saw a lot of people in a very short time."

"Who's first?"

"Browning. He was at my office from 5:30 to 5:45 at the most."

"Okay. When does he get to Carol's apartment?"

"Direct, maybe five after six. If he stopped for a drink, or to make some phone calls maybe 6:15. No. Quinn got there about five after, and Browning came just after that, according to Quinn. Make that not later than 6:10.''

"That gives us a bit of a gap."

"Forget the gap. You phoned me at 5:38, I glanced at my watch. Carol called just before, you said. But she didn't actually get to your place until around 6:25 or later because I got there at 6:35 and she hadn't been there long. So what was she doing during those forty-five or fifty minutes?"

"She had to walk to her place."

"Twenty minutes at the most."

"She walked up and down the block looking for her husband's car and making sure it wasn't there. She got the key" — he held up his hand to prevent an interruption — "and then she stood across the street —"

"She says."

" — for some time getting up her nerve to go upstairs."

"And Quinn still isn't sure just when he saw her."

Murdock considered this. "Did you tell him who his hippie was?"

"It knocked him over. He's going to think some more . . . Okay. And according to Frank, the Colorado license—the stepbrother, you think?—arrived around 6:45 and stayed maybe five minutes . . . Alan Hubbard at maybe seven for another five minutes. Got that?"

"Got it," Murdock said. "And you found Browning at 7:30 and Grayson showed up ten minutes later."

"Right. So what've you got?"

Murdock handed back the notebook with his neatly printed timetable covering nearly a page. Fenner read:

Browning-Fenner . . . 5:30-5:45 . . . Apt. 6:00-6:15?
Quinn . . . Apt. 6:05 plus.
Carol . . . Phone 5:35 . . . Murdock's 6:25 . . . Her apt. ??????
Stepbrother . . . Apt. 6:45-6:50?
Hubbard . . . Apt. 7:00-7:05?
Fenner . . . Leave office 6:10? . . . Murdock's 6:35 . . . Apt. 7:30.
Grayson . . . Apt. 7:40.

The open hot roast beef sandwiches with gravy and whipped potatoes arrived as Fenner pocketed his notebook and pen, and as if by common agreement further discussion was postponed. Even over their coffee and cigarettes the talk was desultory as each stayed busy with his thoughts. It was not until they were back in Fenner's car that Murdock started to question him.

"You did a lot of work for Carol. All of it on Browning, working up divorce evidence?"

"I checked out some people she knew. I asked her why and she said she just wanted to know."

"What do you think the reason was?"

"In the case of Carter and Alan Hubbard, she likes them. It could be she's toying with the idea of maybe marrying one of them someday. Her only interest in Hubbard, since she knew all about his background, was to see if he had any other steady girl friends."

"Did he?"

"No. Dates, yes. He's a damn attractive guy, he's got money and background: he's A-1 marriage material. As a guess I'd say he's still in love with Carol. He'd take her to lunch frequently. Now and then to dinner or a show. He'd take her home but never went up with her. The Puritan in him, I guess, even though she'd been his wife.

"Carter had no particular affair going for him. You probably know his background better than I do. He came to the *Courier* from the West Coast and she wasn't interested in that. She dated him occasionally and he'd go up afterwards once in a while, but he was never up there for longer than it would take to have a friendly nightcap. I guess you know he likes to gamble—hockey games, football, the ponies. He must be doing okay to drive that Mercedes 230SL."

"It's two years old. He got it secondhand."

"They don't give 'em away. And she must have liked him to let him use that place on the Cape to work on his book weekends." He hesitated as his mind reviewed his reports. "She was interested in her Uncle Lamont too."

"She had to know about that blonde he's keeping," Murdock said. "What's her name? Mona something."

"Vail . . . Sure. And Carol was a little surprised when I found out how much it was costing him a month to keep her happy."

"From Las Vegas, wasn't she?"

"Right. Grayson met her out there when he went to visit Carol on that dude ranch. He went there originally to talk her out of marrying Browning, but he spent some time in the casinos and Mona was dealing blackjack. He introduced her to Carol. I don't know if he brought her back, sent for her, or if she just followed him later knowing she had him hooked."

"What's she figure to get out of it? His wife won't divorce him, will she?"

"Well, for a looker like her, with a hood for a one-time boyfriend, dealing for a living, I'd say she's doing okay. She should be socking plenty away from that monthly check she's getting."

There was a note of honest admiration in Murdock's reply. "Man," he said, "you really did a job."

Fenner nodded as he watched the traffic, pleased but not wanting it to show.

"Well, Carol wanted to know and she didn't care what it cost. On that basis I could probably find out the last time you went to bed with a dame."

Murdock laughed and said: "What about Browning? Or is that confidential?"

"Not any more, it isn't. I didn't go back beyond the dude ranch but I found out he'd been a movie and TV extra in horse operas because he could ride; sold used cars on the side. With his looks and build a lot of dames were pushovers, and when he found out Carol was loaded he sort of grabbed her on the rebound. Since she kicked him out he's been living at the University Club."

"I know."

"He also has a snug little love nest for extracurricular activities."

"Oh?"

"In that apartment building next to his wife's. He's down in their rent books as George Bancroft."

"Any special girl friends?"

"One. I'd let you guess but you'd never get it in a million years . . . Lamont Grayson's confidential secretary. Sort of a once-a-month session but she's always out of there by three or four in the morning."

Murdock thought it over, troubled but not knowing why. "What's in it for her?"

"That," said Fenner, doing some thinking of his own, "I don't know but I'll guess for you. She's twenty-six and could have been a virgin. Glasses, sort of plain-looking but pretty eyes, good figure. She's got to know Browning is going to get divorced and probably will get some settlement. So he'd soon be available. With that set-up he'd have no trouble conning her into thinking she could be the next Mrs. Browning."

"Would he go to all that trouble just to get her in bed?"

The same thought had occurred to Fenner when he had been working on the case and he had finally come up with an answer that, while purely speculative, could be made to fit. Never having put it into words, he tried it out now.

"If you knew what it cost Grayson each month to keep things running on his scale of living you might wonder where he got the dough. As far as I know he had no money of his own. The brother, Carol's father, did not mention him in the will but named him co-executor and trustee. Well, by law a trustee is entitled to a fee. I understand it varies from state to state. He doesn't practice any more but he does manage the estates of two other well-off widows, which also bring fees.

"Now those fees," he said, "are based on the value of these estates and Carol's trust. Investment trust fees, for example, vary from around one half of one percent to, in some cases, two percent of the assets. Say he got one. Carol's trust will come between two and three million. Split the difference and Grayson is getting, say, twenty-five grand a year. As an educated guess I think the other two are about a million apiece, which gives in another twenty thousand. Forty-five for him altogether; call it fifty."

"So?" Murdock said.

"He gives that wife in Vermont a grand a month. He writes a check for Mona Vail for fifteen hundred. That's thirty thousand. I wonder if he can live the way he does on what's left. Because fifty, if it is fifty, is before taxes, right?"

"In other words," Murdock said thoughtfully, "you think maybe he's been digging into Carol's trust."

"Well, it's possible, isn't it? And this

confidential secretary Browning's been laying would have access to all records. If there were two sets of books she'd know about it."

Murdock said: "Hmmm—" Then: "And Grayson has to dissolve Carol's trust and hand it over next week."

"Correct."

"Which could mean that if Browning was about to put the bite on Grayson in return for his silence—always assuming that there's anything wrong, and we don't know that there is—then Mr. Lamont Grayson could have sweet motive for murder."

"Also correct. Except for one little detail: Frank Quinn can't put him on the scene at the right time."

9

Alice Maxwell's three-room walk-up was on the third floor of a decaying but respectable four-story red-brick building. Located three blocks beyond the medical school and in a neighborhood no longer as desirable as it was once, it became ideal for a girl who wanted her intern-fiance to be within walking distance whenever he had some free time.

Jack Fenner, Carol Browning's suitcase in hand, was puffing slightly as he came to a stop at the proper door, Murdock at his heels. He knocked three times and presently a none-too-confident voice said: "Who is it?"

When he answered, the door opened a crack and a large hazel eye peered uncertainly at him. Then Carol Browning stepped back to welcome them with a quick smile and an enormous sigh of relief.

"You brought it," she said delightedly, her eyes in that moment only for the bag. "Lovely. Put it anywhere . . . Hello, Kent."

Barefoot, her blond hair pulled back and caught with a ribbon and bow, she was wearing pajamas, very tight across the chest, with the bottoms six inches too short. The robe, also short, was more adequate and she wore both without embarrassment. The bed-sofa had been opened and made ready, and she had the bag open as soon as Fenner got out of the way, little squeals of delight accompanying the deft movements as she emptied it.

"A dress, a sweater-and-skirt outfit, a blouse. Stockings, bras, underwear, a nightgown and robe, even slippers . . . Oh, Jack —"

She grabbed him, arms around his neck and cheek against his, still unselfconscious, and gave him an impulsive hug. She was a big girl, and strong, and Fenner liked the way she felt. She stepped back almost as quickly as she had embraced him.

"How could you know what a girl would want?"

"I was married once."

"Oh, yes," she said, instantly contrite. "Sorry. I'd forgotten." Then, sweeping up an armful of clothes, she said: "I'll be right back."

Fenner watched her open the door of the adjoining bedroom, turned back to Murdock and shrugged. Murdock spread his hands in an answering gesture, dropped them. When he had fanned back his topcoat, he sat down in a straight-backed chair in front of a table-desk, dark eyes troubled and full of doubt.

"Who's going to tell her?"

"You've known her longer," Fenner said, trying to evade responsibility.

"But she was your client; so was her husband."

Carol came back then in a gown and robe that fitted her. "Alice is still asleep. She knew you'd be coming and that I had to wait up, so she went to bed early."

"Fine," Fenner said. "Let's sit down, hunh."

"I'd offer you a drink" — she sat down on the edge of the bed, wrapping her skirts in back of her legs — "but Alice doesn't have a drop in the place . . . Well," she added, frowning now as though sensing some reluctance on the part of both her callers to speak, "is the news good or bad?"

Fenner knew it was up to him but his reply was both reluctant and evasive. "Some good, mostly bad."

"Does someone else know where I am?"

"Only Frank Quinn so far."

"That lawyer in your office? How could he possibly know?"

"I told him."

"You what?" she said, her gaze suddenly stormy. She would have said more but Fenner cut her off, his tone flat and quietly incisive.

"I'll tell you why if you'll keep your cool. Do you want to listen or argue?"

Carol Browning was not used to being spoken to in such tones. For a second or two she seemed undecided and her scowl hinted of some potential rebellion. Finally she gave a twitch of a shoulder, her expression one of forced tolerance. "All right," she said sulkily. "I'm listening."

"Your husband came to my office —"

"I saw him."

"—and asked for my help. He told me

where you'd been and why. I had no more idea where you were then—even when Kent phoned he told me nothing—than he did. When I took the job the obvious place to start was your apartment. I had to have it watched from then on in case you showed up there. Frank Quinn has worked for me before—I'm sure you've met him—and he was the only one I had who could identify you, and that's why I sent him. As a matter of fact he did identify you but at the time he thought you were some hippie."

"Oh—"

"Exactly. He saw you leave the place—apparently after you'd ducked upstairs for that cash you wanted—but he didn't pay too much attention to the time because of that hippie get-up."

"All right." She fidgeted with her hands and shoulders, her impatience beginning to show. "What else?"

"He also saw some other people who were looking for you."

"Is that supposed to be good news?"

"Not exactly. But after what happened I'd say you can stop worrying about going back to Ufford."

"I can? Oh, that's wonderful, Jack. That's the good news? How did you—" She stopped, the quick smile of relief fading as some new concern made itself felt. "What's the bad news?"

Fenner let her have it then, knowing no other way, his tone even, controlled and compassionate.

"When I walked in at 7:30 to pack your bag, your husband was on the floor of the living room with two bullets in his chest. He'd been dead, according to the medical examiner, between one and two hours."

She made no sound as the impact of that statement made itself felt, but seemed somehow to be holding her breath. The hazel eyes opened wide, but slowly, and with disbelief, while the shock began to show and the color left her cheeks. She put the fingertips of both hands to her half-open lips and pressed hard as her gaze moved to Murdock and back.

"Oh, God!" she whispered finally, speaking through her fingers. "Shot? George?"

She lowered her hands, made fists of them, and tucked them between her thighs, clamping her knees tightly as she rocked slightly forward. After another long silent moment she looked up, her eyes sick, the fingermarks still imprinted on her mouth.

Fenner watched the slow transformation of her features. He could actually see them crumble as the shock was transformed slowly into the realization that the information just presented had other meanings beyond the fact of homicide. He could feel Murdock's dark gaze boring into him and understood his silence just as he knew the rest of it was his job, that no help could be expected. He felt a moment of deep sympathy for this girl, but he also understood it had no place in the present scheme of things, since there were other questions he had to ask if he was to be of any help.

"And I guess the police think I did it," she said now. "Is that it?"

"Any wife is a suspect when her husband is murdered, and it won't take them long to learn that you'd had trouble, that you'd kicked him out, that he'd had you committed to Ufford —"

"They know about that?"

"I had to tell them. There was already a bulletin out on you. I had to explain what I was doing at your place and who I was working for. Luckily I had that letter and check from your husband I showed you."

He digressed to tell her about Lamont Grayson, who, he said, was as shocked by her commitment as he had been. He spoke briefly of the police questioning and let it go at that.

"I told you Quinn had seen others come to that building. One guy had a Colorado license on his car. Murdock thinks it could be your stepbrother."

"Barry?"

"That would be Barry Grayson?"

"Yes, he took my father's name."

"What would he be doing in this part of the country?"

"He has some money coming next week. Twenty percent of the estate . . . He came back from Europe—or was it the Caribbean—about a year ago," she added with no further prompting. "He hadn't much money left and he had this chance to open a night club or restaurant or something out in Denver—he'd been to hotel school in Switzerland—and he asked me for a loan. He wrote to Uncle Lamont but he wouldn't advance him anything. I happened to have a healthy checking balance at the time so I let him have twenty thousand. About a month ago he wrote to say if he could get another fifty he could buy his partner out. I suppose he came east early and was looking for me."

"Alan Hubbard came looking for you too," Fenner said.

She nodded, the sag still in her shoulders, her expression dispirited, almost disinterested.

"I'm not surprised. Alan's still in love with me. He'd be worried when he couldn't get in touch with me."

"But you wouldn't call him from Ufford and ask for help."

"I told you why."

"Sure," Fenner said dryly. "The old pride. Did he ever have any trouble with your husband? You must have told him something about what it was like and how George was treating you."

"They had some words one night in a night club. Alan knocked him down."

129

"He also knew you were at Ufford."

"He did? How?"

Fenner explained how Sam Carter and Hubbard had come to his office just as he was about to leave. He said he couldn't see any harm in telling them both that he was working for Browning and why.

"And speaking of Sam Carter," he said. "He was out in front of your apartment building when the police let me go—along with Murdock. I told him what happened and we let him listen when Frank Quinn told me about your callers."

He glanced at Murdock who must have known what he was leading up to, but all Murdock did was shrug with his eyebrows and shake his head. Murdock, it seemed, was quite content to be a spectator on this occasion. He took a small breath and turned back to the girl.

"Your husband was killed with two shots from a .22-caliber revolver; it was there on the floor where someone had dropped it. There was also a .38 that had been fired once at somebody. Carter told us the .22 was registered in his name. He had another gun but bought this extra one to carry when he began digging up dope for that crimes series he was going to write. He said he gave it to you for self-protection when your husband started to get rough and nasty."

"He did."

"You'll tell the police that?"

"Why not? Sam told the truth, why shouldn't I?"

"When did your husband start to get rough?"

"He was always rough, but only once in a while at first. I told myself I was probably as much to blame as he was when we didn't get along. I never did have a very even disposition. I knew then that it was my fault that Alan and I broke up. That time it was pure bitchiness on my part and I guess I still felt guilty."

"When did he start to threaten you?"

"After I told him that you had all those reports and things, and what I intended to do as soon as I got my inheritance. I had to get a court order to get him out of the house. He almost broke the door down once."

"All right." Fenner again glanced at Murdock and this time he got a nod of encouragement, as though Murdock was egging him on and was giving tacit approval to the way he was working. "He told me you'd flipped — and you confirmed that you were pretty gassed out — and that was why he called Dr. Garic. Do you know why he insisted on Ufford instead of some private place?"

"Of course I do!"

The answer both surprised and encouraged Fenner. "Why?"

"I had already told him that when I got my money I'd pay him one hundred thousand when I divorced him just for his nuisance value. I could afford it and I didn't want any trouble."

"And?"

"He came to the hospital, I think it was Monday. I was all right then, I mean mentally, but I was very damn furious with him for committing me there. I asked him why and he said a hundred thousand for a settlement wasn't enough, not with what I had coming. If I'd make it two he'd see that I got released in a couple of days. I told him to go to hell."

Fenner believed her. Spoiled or not, she

had spunk. She also, he thought, could be a very difficult woman to handle. Experience had taught him that nearly everyone had within himself the capacity for murder, given the proper provocation, a factor that varied with the individual. More husbands had been killed while beating or abusing their wives than for any other reason and that possibility could well have presented itself if Browning had walked in on his wife unexpectedly while she had come to get the cash she needed. Right now he knew there was still an unpleasant question or two that had to be asked.

"Did you tell the truth about what you did at your apartment?"

"Of course I did!" she said, annoyance showing for the first time and the hazel eyes resentful.

"You haven't seen your husband since his visit to Ufford?"

"No."

"You didn't shoot him with that little .22?"

"Damn you, Jack Fenner—"

"Hold it, hold it!" Fenner yelled, not minding the outburst because he was already prepared for such a reaction. "Get used to that question, Carol," he said flatly. "You're going to be asked it over and over again. By Homicide, by the D.A.'s office, by other detectives, maybe working in teams. Now about Ufford," he went on hurriedly to keep her quiet.

"All you have to do is phone your uncle in the morning. From here. You don't have to tell him where you are. Tell him to see this Dr. Garic and explain the situation. He can get in touch with the hospital people, ask them to send a release to Grayson, and that will be that. You should be more concerned right now about the District Attorney because his subpoena will take precedence over the Ufford commitment anyway."

"You mean I'm going to be arrested?" she said, some new feeling of consternation at once apparent.

"No. But you'll have to go to his office, or headquarters . . . Look, Carol." He leaned forward, his manner at once reasonable, his voice quiet and confidential. "They know you're missing. They know you've been at Ufford. If they don't already know, they'll find out you've had trouble with your husband. It's a cinch they'll be questioning the super of those two buildings and he's going to tell them you came for a key to your apartment; maybe he can pin the time down and maybe he can't.

"In my opinion," he said in that same even voice, "and I think Kent will agree, the thing for you to do when the time comes is to call your uncle and arrange a meeting so you can go to the D.A.'s office together."

He leaned back, watching her, satisfied that she was accepting his logic and advice, knowing that this was the time to suggest a warning and a favor.

"One more thing. You can make a lot of headaches for Kent and me if you tell anyone about our part in this little disappearance. It might even be wiser from our point of view if you didn't even tell your uncle. It's nobody's business but ours."

This time she smiled at him, a small smile but somehow reassuring.

"Don't give it another thought. You've helped enough, and believe me I'm grateful. But since you're doing the coaching just what do I say when they ask me where I've been?"

"You refuse to answer, which, as they say, is your constitutional right. You turn yourself in with your attorney and let him take it from there. Refusing to answer a question in a preliminary investigation is no offense; Grayson won't let them bully you."

As he finished and leaned back he heard Murdock clear his throat. He cocked a brow at him and said: "All right, oracle, are you ready to enter the discussion?"

"The discussion," Murdock said with quiet good humor, "has been very interesting indeed. Just one question, if I may . . . When exactly does she turn herself over to Grayson and the D.A.? Not tonight."

"Hell no!"

He made himself think, weighing one alternative against another. He felt strangely tired and wanted very much to have a drink as soon as possible. When he could come up with no positive and definite answer he said so.

"I don't know. Maybe tomorrow, maybe not. I want to nose around a bit. I have a date with Sergeant Gaynor in the morning at his office." He let the grin come. "Something about a statement. I'll pick his brains and see what they know at headquarters. I'll keep in touch."

"Then I'm to stay here, correct?" the girl said, some disappointment showing.

"As the old Duke Ellington piece says, 'Do Nothing 'Till You Hear From Me' . . . When you see Alice in the morning, tell her you'll be staying and that she is to say nothing to anyone until she sees me at the office. Okay?"

He rose then, feeling his bones creak a little. After glancing from one to the other, Carol came to her feet, folding her robe about her, clasped arms hugging her breasts. She stood that way as they buttoned their coats. She said she couldn't thank them enough and they said not to try. Moving to the door with them, she said she felt tired and beaten and all used up inside but would Fenner please call her as soon as he could and tell her what she should do.

10

Sergeant Joe Gaynor's office was on the fourth floor of the headquarter's building, and when Jack Fenner walked into the squad room just before ten the next morning he found Gaynor at his desk, one of eight in a two-windowed scruffy-looking room whose equipment consisted of the desks, typewriters, and an extra straight-backed oak chair beside each desk. There was only one other detective working his machine at the time and Fenner was relieved to find Captain Lane's door closed.

"About time," Gaynor said without irritation. "I was about to have them bring you in."

Fenner sat down in the extra chair and let the comment pass. He had had his session with Alice Maxwell in his office and was confident that she would do the right thing if questioned. He had told her about the truck driver named Megan who was expected to call, instructing her to take fifteen dollars out of the office cash and give it to Megan after inspecting Carol's wedding ring.

Now, as ready as he ever would be for Gaynor, he said: "What do you know that I don't?"

"Hah!" said Gaynor. "First things first." He pushed two sheets, in triplicate, across the desk. "Read it. See if it covers the essentials. Any minor changes you can ink in and initial. If you don't like it we can get a stenographer in and start over."

Fenner skimmed the typewritten lines of the statement, said it was close enough, and signed all three copies.

Gaynor gathered them. "This will do for now. Some assistant D.A. who isn't so trustful may want a verbatim version."

"So how about letting me in on your progress."

"Why?"

"I told you—or Lane—last night. I've got a dead client. I may never get paid but I'd like to keep my hand in just as a matter of principle."

"Principle, hunh?" Gaynor leaned back and yawned. "That's not the why I had in mind. I meant why should we tell you anything? You're private now. You take down more in a year than Lane and I put together, right?"

"Could be," Fenner said noncommittally.

"So let us cops handle it."

"Oh?" Fenner's smile was thin and the dark-green eyes narrowed slightly. "It's like that, is it?"

"Just like that."

"Okay." Fenner leaned forward, palms on kneecaps as though preparing to rise. "Then you don't care about what Frank Quinn learned while he had the Browning place staked out last night from around six o'clock on. Fine. I'll work my end of the street and you can have yours."

Gaynor blinked, uncertain now. "Wait a minute!" He fidgeted in his chair, his embarrassment showing as he realized he had boxed himself in. He glanced at Lane's door, ran his tongue over his teeth. "Quinn was working for you? What did he tell you?"

"He said there were apparently some callers at that address."

"Like who?"

It was Fenner's turn to shake his head. His grin remained fixed, so did the cool and challenging look in his eyes.

"No dice, Joe. You laid out the rules and you're stuck with them."

Gaynor spread his hands. "I could bend them a little."

"How far?"

"That depends on what you've got."

"That's a little indefinite, isn't it? We trade or we don't."

"I'll make a deal."

"I'm still listening."

"You tell me something we don't already know and I'll give you a fact or two you probably don't have."

"Not some techinal crap your boys turned up because, frankly, I doubt if they've got a damn thing that will help."

"It's a little better than that. How about it? You first."

Fenner had already made up his mind. His stalling was just part of an act and he wasn't worried about the sergeant's reneging. For he knew Gaynor was an honest, hard-working detective, conscientious and fair. He had too much integrity and self-respect to weasel on a promise willingly given. That Gaynor might also have some honest respect for his present adversary did not enter Jack Fenner's mind.

"A Caddy convertible that didn't belong there stopped for a few minutes while the owner went in. It had a Colorado license."

"What the hell good is that? You got the number?"

"Quinn has."

"So?"

"From what I've learned—never mind where—the driver comes from Denver. I think his last name is Grayson. A phone call to Denver authorities ought to turn him up in a very few minutes."

He finished, intent on his words, before he realized that Gaynor had a broad smile on his face, the Irish-blue eyes sparkling with amusement.

"What the hell is so funny?"

"I was just thinking. I'm beginning to see

142

how you get away with those fat fees I hear you're collecting."

"Hunh?"

"What I mean is you think real good when you put your mind to it. The only reason we don't act on your suggestion is that *we already know* this guy's name is Barry Grayson and that he's now staying at the Walker House. Been here four days. Stepbrother of the Browning dame."

Fenner heard every word but it took a moment to put them together. Gaynor, pleased with the reaction, chuckled softly but he was not a man to gloat over a small advantage.

"You see," he said. "The guy came in about a half hour ago. Asked Information who he should see, said he wanted to discuss the Browning murder. Information sent him up here."

It was Fenner's turn to grin and this time it was genuine. "Round one for you, Joe."

"Seems he read about it in the paper and was willing to admit being there to learn more about just what happened. Said he'd gone up about" — he shuffled some papers, found what he wanted — "ten of seven. He'd

143

been trying to get in touch with the stepsister, Browning's wife, by phone and decided to go and see for himself. Pushed the buzzer a few times, tried the door. He was going to ask the janitor to open up but didn't know how to find him. Does this check out with Quinn's information?"

It was Fenner's turn to consult his notebook. "It does."

"So you see, old buddy, since you haven't told me anything, I don't owe you anything. Right? You want to try again?"

"Sure," Fenner said, warming up to the game. "Right after Grayson there was another caller. Her ex-husband. Name of Hubbard," he added, aware that he had Gaynor's attention. "Alan Hubbard."

"Would that be the investment company Hubbard on State Street?"

"It would."

"What about him?"

"She was married to him before Browning."

"Oh, ho! Do you think he could still be carrying a torch?"

"Could be."

"Any bad feeling that you know of?"

"I understand there was. They had some words in a night club some time back—don't ask me where—and Hubbard decked the husband."

"You got some times?" He made notes as Fenner spoke; then said: "Stayed only five minutes or so if Quinn's right? Came along after the Denver fellow? . . . Okay, you got one coming. Try this on for size."

He leaned back in his battered swivel chair, the ancient springs protesting.

"Did you know that the Browning dame was wearing a hippie get-up?"

"How the hell would I know?" Fenner said innocently in an effort to disguise some new inner disturbance.

"Must have switched from the outfit she walked away from Ufford in. Not bad," he said in open admiration. "I understand she was a blond good-looking doll, so who'd be looking for a hippie? Neat, hunh?"

"How do you know all this?"

"This department sees all, knows all . . . No," Gaynor added, serious now, "it was actually pretty simple. You know the routine when someone is knocked off in an apartment. Question the neighbors. Well *her* neighbors didn't know a damn thing. Old building, thick walls, most of them out. So we go next door and talk to the super—he handles both buildings—and he tells us about this hippie who showed up around six—he's not sure about the time—and asks for a duplicate key to the Browning apartment. He's about to toss her out when she yanks off this fright wig she's wearing and it's Mrs. Browning. Said something about a masquerade, which he don't buy, but what the hell, he has to give her a key, don't he?"

That was a lot of talk for Gaynor and he seemed rather pleased with himself.

"So it comes right back to the wife, wouldn't you say? We can put her on the scene at the right time, she had all the motive we'll ever need—"

Fenner interrupted with a question that stopped the detective and steered him onto another track.

"What about that little .22?"

"Hah! This should grab you good. That little gun was registered. You know to who?"

"Sam Carter."

Fenner spoke casually, almost with

indifference, and he enjoyed the effect that he had on Gaynor, who sat up straight, jaw sagging and disbelief in his wide-open stare.

"Now how the hell would you know that?"

"Simple. He told me. Me and Kent Murdock and Frank Quinn."

"Told you? When?"

"Last night after Lane said I could shove off. Quinn was still parked across the street on his stake-out and I went over to get a report."

"How did Murdock get there? You mean he was with that gang of news guys outside on the walk? I thought he was the inside boss at the *Courier* these days."

"He is, most of the time. The way I get it their man in the pressroom at headquarters gave the office a call. Carter and Murdock happened to be in, Carter in the city room and Murdock in his little cubby," he said, making up his story as he went along. "It's got a radio to keep in touch with the company cars. I guess he heard the flash. He talked to a car with a camera and sent the guy to that address, but he came too because he's an old friend of Mrs. Browning and he wanted to know the score."

Fenner took a small breath, a little amazed that he could lie so easily. "Carter's a friend too; he's also their best crime reporter—"

"I know that."

"So naturally they wanted to know what I knew and why I was in the apartment in the first place. We sort of drifted over to Quinn's car while he told me what he'd seen, and in telling the others what I knew I said a .22 had been the murder weapon. Carter damn near popped his cork. He said it was his gun, that he'd loaned it to Mrs. Browning after her husband had tried to break the door down one night. Did he come in or did you go after him when you'd checked the gun registration?"

"He came in last night. I think he'd had a few belts but he was still jumpy. His story checks with yours. What we want to know when we get the woman is, Will she verify Carter's story about that gun?" Gaynor stopped, thinking hard, brows furrowed and eyes all screwed up.

"We didn't know he was a friend of the dame's. How good a friend? And how come? I mean a rich broad like that and a reporter?"

"I think Murdock introduced them and they seemed to hit it off," Fenner said, glad to be telling the truth for a change as he went on to explain about the lunches and dinners and the shooting shack on the Cape Carter was using weekends. Gaynor nodded when Fenner finished, his eyes still full of thought as he pondered this new information.

"Yeah," he said finally. "That's one I owe you. Because if Mrs. Browning denies Carter's story he could be in a bit of a bind. His gun, maybe bad feeling with the husband we don't know about. Browning was sort of nasty and violent at times from what we've learned so far. He could have gone up there, couldn't he? Carter?"

"Not unless he went up the back way."

"You mean Quinn would have seen him."

"That's what he was getting paid for. Have you checked the back way? There is one, isn't there?"

"It was locked, but no key. It could have been picked I guess, and a lad who's the crime expert for the *Courier* has got to know at least one lock man."

He leaned back, dismissing that line of thought. "But first we find the dame, and we will."

"You got a warrant out?"

"Just a wanted-for-questioning-six-state bulletin. We staked out the Back Bay and South Stations, the airport, bus stations. Nothing yet. She's holed up somewhere in the city is my guess, so we're working on all hotels, known rooming houses, motels. It could take time but that we got . . . So Carter was a good friend, hunh?" he added in an abrupt digression. "Is that right about the Syndicate boys sending him threatening letters?"

"Did he report them?"

"Not here. It's just a rumor but—"

"And one that happens to be true."

"You see any of 'em."

"Murdock did. You know the kind. Block letters cut out of newspaper or magazine headlines. Also there was at least one phone call to the office. Carter signaled to a rewrite man who overheard most of it on an extension."

He stood up and Gaynor rose with him.

"The word is around that you did a lot of work for the Browning woman. That right? Divorce evidence, that sort of thing?"

"Mostly, but not entirely."

"You'd know her pretty well by now I guess. Personally? Ever take her out?"

"To lunch."

"On business?"

"We discussed business if that's what you mean . . . But maybe you'd better tell me just what's bugging you."

"I was thinking," Gaynor said, his glance oblique and very quiet of manner now, "that here's a woman in one hell of a lot of trouble. She could be a candidate for murder one, probably is or she'd have got in touch with that lawyer uncle of hers, whatever the hell his name is, and come in with him like any responsible citizen."

"So."

"I guess you did a good job for her, you usually do. By now she has faith in you, trusts you. She's in a jam and she needs all the help she can get. She might get in touch with you, hunh?"

"It's possible."

"She's got the kind of money that can

hire the best lawyers in the business. If she escaped from Ufford there could be a mental angle that might be useful as a defense; there might even have been provocation." He raised his index finger. "Mind you, I don't know if she killed the guy or not, but she's got to come up with an awful lot of answers. You ought to keep in mind that helping her stay lost could get your license suspended, maybe permanently." He smiled thinly. "Then what would you do?"

"Well," Fenner said, "I wasn't fired from the force, I resigned." He winked. "I guess maybe I'd just have to put in for reinstatement."

11

The information Sergeant Gaynor had given Fenner about Carol Browning, as a hippie asking the building superintendent for a key, was not surprising since Fenner, aware of the thoroughness of such police investigations, had expected some such news. What was helpful was the hotel address, the Walker House, of the Colorado stepbrother.

Having filed this in the back of his mind for future reference, he went back to the office to consult his files since there was someone he wanted to see first. He asked Alice Maxwell if the truck driver with the wedding ring had shown up and she opened the center drawer of her desk and produced it. He took a moment to admire the handsome platinum-and-diamond band before he slipped it into the change pocket of his jacket.

"Did he say anything?"

"He just asked if I had fifteen dollars for him."

"Good enough. Now will you check the phone book and see if you can find a Mona Vail listed. She lives at the Riverside Arms."

Once in the inner office and rid of his topcoat, he unlocked the steel filing cabinet and took out an inch-thick folder which held the onionskin carbons of earlier reports. He opened it until he found the pertinent sheets and began to make notes as he boned up on his subject.

When the buzzer sounded and Alice announced that Mona Vail was in the book he asked her to call and see if she was in.

"If she is, tell her that a friend of a friend named Fenner would like to call her apartment in a half hour or so. Ask if it would be convenient for her to see me . . . Oh, and Alice, has Frank been in?"

"No."

"Well, if he calls tell him Sergeant Gaynor is probably going to want to see him. Maybe Gaynor has already been in touch, but tell Frank anyway."

He took his time jotting down a few notes

as reference points while he rounded out a mental picture of Lamont Grayson's mistress. He had about finished when Alice buzzed him to say Miss Vail would expect him.

The Riverside Arms was one of the older and more expensive apartment buildings in the area. It was aptly named since those who could afford it occupied the river apartments with an excellent view up and down the river with its handsome bridges. There was a doorman, a marquee, a bored reception clerk who doubled on the switchboard, a uniformed elevator operator. When the clerk had relayed Fenner's name to the proper apartment, he nodded, still bored, and said:

"You can go right up. Apartment 4-C. The elevator man will show you where."

The woman who opened the door for him was something to see, a tinted blond with an opulent figure and striking green eyes that had been mascara'd and shadowed by someone who knew how. She wore snug pink slacks that molded nicely her hips and thighs and the blouse was flimsy enough to hint at proud well-shaped breasts.

The green eyes looked right at him in those first seconds, taking in the overall picture before focusing on his face. There was a half smile that seemed somehow approving and he wondered if it was him or just a habit she had when regarding all new men.

"Mr. Fenner?" she asked in a lazy throaty voice. "Come in, please."

She let him into the entryway but when the door closed she was not yet ready to let him get beyond that point.

"Your secretary, or whoever it was that called, said you were a friend of a friend. Who might that be?"

"The best friend you've got."

"Oh?" she said, the first shadow of doubt flicking in her glance.

"Lamont Grayson."

"You're a friend of his?"

"I lied a little," Fenner said, innocently and trying to look a bit embarrassed. "I've met him."

"But he didn't send you?"

"Oh, no," he said in perish-the-thought accents. "I'm here on business."

"Fuzz?"

"Ex-fuzz," he said easily as he took out his wallet and displayed a photostat of his license.

Some doubt still lingered while she held a quick debate with herself, tipping her head a half inch to one side, the green eyes still amused and faintly mocking as she decided in his favor.

Finally, with the faintest of shrugs, she stood aside to let him pass, following him into a long, tastefully furnished living room whose two large windows overlooked the river. In that first inclusive glance, Fenner was impressed. Several pieces looked like genuine antiques, the odd tables, the breakfront, a handsome maple highboy. The wall-to-wall carpet was a pastel green and an inch thick; the divan had enormous cushions with a made-to-order look.

"Nice," he said, turning back to her as she settled herself on the divan and pointed to a matching club chair near one end. "Furnish it yourself?"

"Lamont helped . . . Sit down, Mr. Fenner. I take it this isn't an official call."

"A friendly one, I hope."

"I hope so too. And since I get the idea

this may turn out to be somewhat personal how about a drink? Or is it too early for you?"

"It is, a little," Fenner said, a glance at his watch telling him it still was a half hour to noon. "But if you feel like one I'll be happy to join you."

"Good," she said, pointing, "over there. A Scotch on the rocks please, with a touch of water."

Over there proved to be a handsome cellaret, one of the few modern pieces in the room. The cupboard part was well filled with every manner of alcoholic beverage, the top disclosed glasses and an ice bucket that looked recently filled.

"Ice even," he said, selecting two glasses.

"It's one of my daily chores. In case Lamont should decide to drop in around lunchtime."

As he made the drinks he glanced idly about, noticing now the Governor Winthrop desk that stood several feet away. Its lid was down revealing an expensive-looking desk set on which lay a longish folder with the trademark of an airline on its cover. He recognized the company but that was all, and at the moment it was nothing more than another fact observed and filed away.

He gave her her glass, sat down, raised his duplicate of her drink, said Cheers, and swallowed.

"Now," she said, settling herself with one leg tucked under her bottom and an arm across the back of the divan to accentuate her bust, "just what does Ex-fuzz Mr. Fenner want to talk about?"

"You."

A slight frown began to show. "Have we ever met?"

"No, but I know a lot about you."

"Oh, how?"

"I did a lot of work a while back for Grayson's niece. Do you know her?"

"Not well. You mean Mrs. Browning?"

"Right."

"Divorce stuff?"

"Mainly. But she seemed to want to know things about a lot of her friends, plus a few other people, and she had the money to pay for it."

A frown was fixed now, the green eyes narrowing with suspicion.

"This other people would include me?"

"It would."

"Okay, tell me the story of my life."

"Just the last three years," Fenner said, "You're a West Coast girl, a one-time dancer, blackjack dealer, ex-girl friend of a syndicate hood named Micelli now doing five-to-ten. Grayson met you in Vegas when he was out there to see his niece. Apparently he flipped and made some sort of proposition. However, it was you who came east and he set you up."

She sipped her drink and her tone was faintly sardonic but not yet resentful when she spoke. "Do go on, Mr. Ex-fuzz Fenner."

Fenner grinned, suddenly aware that he liked this woman. There was, he knew, some real down-to-earth toughness here but he guessed that she was smart enough to act the lady when with Grayson and he doubted that she ever would be crude, regardless of the circumstances, when she was in his presence. No heavyweight mentally, she had enough basic female shrewdness to know she had a good thing going and she apparently was not too worried at twenty-seven — or was it twenty-eight? — about the future.

Now he said: "I've been wondering what you do for that fifteen hundred bucks a month?"

She wedged her leg out from under her hip, put both feet on the floor, and swallowed the last of her drink.

"How," she demanded, "would you know about that?"

"Oh, that wasn't too tough" — Fenner gestured emptily with his glass to give the impression that this was nothing but chitchat and of no real importance — "for an old experienced hand like me. To keep your name out of it, Grayson has a check made out each month to the Acme Investment Company. You're it."

"Well, I'll be godamned," she said, her incipient annoyance vanishing in that instant. She gave him a small reluctant smile and handed him the glass. "Once more please . . . You know," she added as she stood up, "you're a very amusing character, Mr. Ex-fuzz Fenner. I think I could get to like you."

"It pays better to like Grayson."

"You know it does," she said, accepting the refill. "And you want to know what I do for his money. One simple thing: I keep little Mona available at all times, which isn't too hard considering. A man of his age isn't too demanding. In fact, he needs a little encouraging from time to time. I provide it."

"But what do you do with yourself the rest of the time?"

"You'd be surprised." She got comfortable again, her manner once more at ease. "Beauty parlor two afternoons a week. Health clinic two other afternoons, believe it or not. After all, a girl with a nice figure should keep it, wouldn't you say? . . . I go to the track once in a while when the weather is nice—"

"Alone?"

"With what Lamont gives me, wouldn't you?"

"You knew he was married when you came east?"

"Sure. I always try to know the score."

"I had an idea you would." He put his empty glass on the coffee table. "Think he's ever going to divorce his wife and marry you?"

She shrugged and her pretty face was relaxed in some moment of reflection. She touched the back of her blond hair absently, looked back at him.

"I hadn't thought too much about it. I have a lovely wardrobe, two fur coats, a couple of nice pieces of jewelry" — she held one hand up to show a handsome emerald-and-diamond cocktail ring — "and each and every month a nice fat sum gets deposited in little Mona's personal account. Hell, if he kicked me out right now I'd have a bigger bank balance than I ever dreamed of. It mounts up, you know, if you sock it away regularly."

Fenner offered a cigarette which was refused, and shifted his emphasis as he lit it.

"Do you know how much he's paying his wife?"

"A thousand a month, as if you didn't know."

"And you probably know he's the trustee for Mrs. Browning's estate, which is probably a fairly profitable operation for him."

"So?"

"Did you know he hands over the estate next week?"

"I think he mentioned something about it."

"That's going to cut hell out of his income."

"Oh, I'm sure he has some plans."

"Is marriage one of them?"

"Who knows. At twenty-seven I've still got time, wouldn't you say?"

"But you don't know these plans," Fenner said, persisting.

"I never pry. Maybe that's one of the reasons he stays sold on me." She yawned lazily, stretched to accent her shapely torso, and came to her feet.

"All I know is that he said something about taking a little trip once he gets that estate out of the way. You know," she added, the half-smile no longer humorous, "I thought I liked you; now I'm not so sure. I mean, you can get pretty boring when you put your mind to it. Just what *did* you come here for, Mr. Ex-fuzz? I'd say you already knew enough about me."

Fenner, standing close to her now and seeing the nice skin and the very expert make-up, decided he still liked this girl, which made him wonder if some vague stirring inside of him could be a form of jealously at Lamont Grayson's good fortune.

He said casually: "Did you know George Browning was murdered last night in his wife's apartment?"

"There was a short piece in this morning's *Courier.*"

"I'm the guy that found him."

The green eyes opened then, her indifference forgotten. "You did? Do the police know who did it?"

"I doubt it. They're looking for the wife, Grayson's niece."

"Well, what do you know. I always heard he was a first-class bastard but—" She let the sentence dangle and tried another question. "How come you found him? What were you doing there?"

"Looking for Mrs. Browning. Browning sent her to the State Hospital at Ufford and she ran away yesterday afternoon. Browning hired me about 5:30 last night to find her . . . Did Grayson tell you he walked in on me just after I'd phoned the police last night?"

"No."

"See him today?"

"No, but I talked to him on the phone. Why?"

"I just wondered. He told the police he'd come there because he was trying to locate his niece. Apparently he didn't know about the Ufford bit until I told him. They asked him to account for his time from 5:30 on last night. He said he'd been with someone most of the time."

She was watching him now, the green eyes speculative but unconcerned. "Did he say who?"

"No. I think the police think it may have been a woman and Grayson didn't deny it. I was wondering if it was you."

She had a half-smile working on the red mouth. "I had an idea you might be kicking some such idea around," she said, "so I'll tell you something." She started for the entrance hall and he had to follow. As she reached the opening she turned to face him, her shaved and penciled brows arching and some mockery in her glance. "Why don't you keep right on wondering, Mr. Ex-fuzz?"

Before Fenner could reply the telephone shrilled its brassy note somewhere in the room, as though to punctuate her reply. She looked back, undecided it seemed, whether to answer it first or show Fenner out. The second ring activated her and she gave an impatient snort as she strode purposefully back toward an inner door. She picked up the instrument after its fourth ring.

She said: "Yes?" and a moment later turned, one hand outstretched. "For you," she added with some surprise.

Fenner came back, took the handset, thanked her.

"Yes, Alice," he said, knowing it could be no one else.

"I'm glad I caught you. I just had a call from a Sergeant Joe Gaynor. He sounded pretty urgent. I said I thought I could reach you and he said you're to meet him right away or he'd send for you."

"At headquarters?"

"No, he gave me an address," she said and repeated it.

He cradled the handset, eyes thoughtful until he noticed the woman waiting at the doorway. He thanked her for the drink and she said she liked company when she drank.

"Stop by again sometime," she said with an odd little smile, "when you're not working."

12

Warner Street, opening on Atlantic Avenue and close to the railroad yards, was a one-block affair of loft buildings and wholesale supply houses, devoted mostly to the construction business. With no retail shops there were few pedestrians on the sidewalks and Fenner, driving by, noticed a police car had blocked off his end of the street. Continuing until he could find a place to park, he walked back to where two uniformed officers prevented entry and detoured traffic.

The huskier of the two seemed familiar, but Fenner could not give him a name so he merely said that Sergeant Gaynor sent for him.

"Yeah," the officer said, "he told us to send you right along when you showed up."

There were no more than a dozen of the curious waiting to see what it was all about, and unlike the night before there were only two representatives of the press: Morris, of the *News,* and Sam Carter. Both moved to intercept him.

"Somebody send for you, Jack?" Carter asked.

"Joe Gaynor."

"Did he tell you what it's about?" Morris said.

"Just that he wanted to see me. What do *you* know?"

"Atkins at headquarters got a flash to investigate an abandoned car."

"Same with me," said Morris. "I guess we both got curious to know why they'd put a routine thing like that on the air." He pointed down the street. "And it looks like our hunches were okay. They don't send an ambulance for an abandoned car."

Fenner started off and Carter kept pace for two steps to say that he'd wait; then Fenner was walking briskly down a block that was mostly in shadow now even in midday. He counted the cluster of cars halfway down: a marked cruiser, an unmarked sedan, a coupe obviously not police, an ambulance, a tow truck. This had been backed up to a plain dark-gray sedan that looked four or five years old.

Not until then did intuition start to work on him and he was conscious first of some strange feeling of apprehension that grew swiftly into a more positive sense of foreboding. Closer now, recognizing the sedan even as he tried to overcome his doubts, he moved on, the bottom dropping slowly out of his stomach and some inner sickness taking its place. He swallowed against it when he saw the license number and noticed the strangely misshapen, blanket-covered figure on the stretcher with the medical examiner's man crouched close by.

Joe Gaynor, who had been watching Fenner approach, stopped him before he got too close and pulled him over to the blank brick wall of a loft building.

"I guess you recognize the car," he said. "No point in looking. It ain't pretty. We had quite a time getting him out from behind the wheel because he'd stiffened up real good. The M.E. thinks it could have happened up to twelve hours ago."

"Frank?" Fenner asked automatically,

still shaky and incredulous and speaking past the thickness in his throat.

"Two slugs in the right side below the armpit."

Fenner took a deep breath to put down the inner nausea and waited a few seconds to get his ragged nerves in hand, to get some control in his voice. Not until he had closed his mind off to the scene he had witnessed could he speak.

"You think it happened here?"

"He was behind the wheel but slumped sideways so you couldn't see him from a passing car. That's why the boys in the cruiser didn't see him. You notice the rear end is sticking out over a foot, which makes it illegal parking, but in a block like this who cares? You can't blame the guys in the car much. They might have stopped for a look eventually, but it was two truck drivers waiting for a load who finally got curious enough to take a peek. They couldn't get in to touch him—keys in the ignition—you don't need a key to lock the doors if you know how. Anyway, they didn't like what they saw and called in."

He watched Fenner with one eye, and

then with both, but Fenner wasn't ready to talk. He got a cigarette going, felt the perspiration in the palms of his hands and wiped them. He kept his glance averted until the doors of the ambulance closed on its grisly burden. Finally, as the tow truck hooked up to the sedan, he swallowed hard to clear his throat.

"I guess he never had a chance."

"I'd say none. Maybe whoever did it held the gun on him and made him drive here; maybe not. He could have parked for a talk, not suspecting anything until the slugs hit him. You got any ideas?"

"Only one," Fenner said wearily. "He must have seen something last night on that stake-out he didn't tell us about."

"He saw the killer," Gaynor said bluntly, "That's who he saw. How else? He made the mistake of holding out, hoping for a pay-off. The guy always was a loser, but as an attorney I'd think he'd be too cagey for that kind of caper."

Fenner felt too discouraged to argue. The sickness still lay heavy on his stomach, but his mind was working now and the thoughts that came to him did little to dispel it so he waited, silent, some hunch warning him that Gaynor hadn't finished. The sergeant confirmed the hunch.

"I've been trying to locate him ever since you stopped by and told me he was working for you. No wonder we couldn't find him. How could an experienced attorney like that be so stupid?"

"He was always hoping for the big break," Fenner said, thinking aloud rather than answering Gaynor. "He was convinced it was there waiting for him just around the corner. He didn't have a mean or vicious bone in his body."

"So let's go over what he told you last night. He saw the stepbrother, then Hubbard, the ex-husband, then Lamont Grayson. I say he had to have seen someone else he held out about."

"Not necessarily."

"How do you figure that?"

"He could have lied about the times," Fenner argued, not really believing it but refusing to consider the alternative. "I can't see a motive for the stepbrother, but Alan Hubbard could have been up there longer than Frank said. Grayson, who could have had motive, could have come earlier, ducked out to set up some sort of alibi and come back to see what was going to happen. It's been done before . . . Well," he demanded, "It's possible, isn't it?"

"Possible," Gaynor said, very sober now and wanting to be fair, "but I can't buy it."

"Then who *did* he see?"

"The Browning woman, who else? She's loaded, isn't she? She could pay off big and Quinn would know it. She walks away from Ufford and disappears. If she's clean, how come nobody's seen her? If she reads the papers she's got to know her husband got knocked off; why hasn't she come in to find out how and why?"

Such questions were hard to answer because the reasoning behind them was sound. There was also something in the sergeant's tone and manner, the positiveness of his belief that made Fenner look at him more closely.

"You got something else, is that it?"

"Yeah, we've got something."

"Why the hell didn't you say so?"

"I wanted to hear your arguments." With that Gaynor reached into a pocket and brought forth a folded slip that looked like a check. As he offered it for Fenner's inspection he said: "We found that in Frank's inside jacket pocket."

It was a check all right, a blank form without personalization or identification number. It was made out to Frank Quinn and signed by Carol Browning in the amount of twenty thousand dollars. The date was October 17.

"That estate of hers," Gaynor said. "She gets it on the fifteenth, right? That's why the check is postdated. By the seventeenth she'd have all the cash she needed for a pay-off."

Fenner looked at the check a long time, not actually seeing it after the first glance, but aware of a new kind of creeping despair as he tried furiously to find a logical answer that could refute this new evidence.

He remembered his talk with Carol the night before and how innocently and convincingly she had argued. He was also detective enough to recall other incidents where guilty women had lied with the same conviction. A guilty Carol could well do the same. What was there to lose?

"Well," Gaynor said, retrieving the

check, "would you say that was her signature?"

"From what I can remember, yes."

"And if we find it in Quinn's pocket she had to give it to him."

Fenner, who had been leaning one shoulder against the wall, straightened and shrugged his coat collar in place. Gaynor's facts seemed unarguable but they could be faulted.

"Let me ask you a question, several questions."

"Shoot."

"You give a guy a check to protect yourself from arrest. You plan to kill him and you figure a good clean way to do it: con him into taking a ride to talk things over, pick a good dark and deserted street, stick a gun into his unsuspecting ribs as he sits at the wheel. Lock him in and take off. Without taking back the check? Come off it, Joe. It just doesn't fit."

"You ever kill a guy like that? Deliberate, cold-blooded—"

"You know I haven't."

"Then how do you know how you'd act? How do you know you wouldn't panic and run before someone came along and maybe saw you? How about a dame that was just out of a mental hospital? A gun going off in a closed car would sound like a cannon. It could panic anybody. Especially a dame who had killed her husband and could only think of setting up the guy who could put the finger on her . . . I say Quinn saw the dame last night and held out on you so he could proposition her for a fat payoff."

Fenner thought it over and knew Gaynor was right in one area. Quinn had seen Carol at her apartment, not knowing at the time who she was until he, Fenner, had pulled him aside at the end of their car-side conference and told him. Not only that, he had told Quinn where Carol was staying. That Quinn had gone to see her sometime after Fenner and Murdock had left Alice Maxwell's apartment could no longer be disputed. Because such thoughts were too discouraging to dwell on, he said:

"Where would she get the gun, Joe? According to you she had already left the gun we know about on her apartment floor. Maybe she just happened to have another in her handbag."

Gaynor, the amusement in his eyes suggesting he was unperturbed by the sarcasm, answered frankly.

"I wouldn't even guess where and how she got a gun. What I do say is that when we pick her up and start working on her, with or without her lawyer, *we'll find out* where she got that gun. It won't be all that tough."

He glanced up and down the block, emptied now of uniformed officers and precinct plainclothesmen. He started to turn toward the unmarked sedan where a driver waited.

"I guess that's it. Except for one thing which you've heard before. She gets in touch with you or you locate her before we do, turn her in, Jack." He winked. "No threat, you understand; just a bit of friendly advice."

Sam Carter was the only one on the corner when Fenner retraced his steps. His plump, intelligent face with its mini-beard and mustache was made even more somber and concerned by the black-rimmed glasses.

"The word I got is the guy in the car was Frank Quinn," he said. "One of the cops said he'd been shot twice, dead for some time according to him."

Fenner nodded, not wanting to talk about it but not wanting to brush the reporter off either.

"Around midnight, the examiner's man thinks."

"They find the gun?"

"If they did, Gaynor didn't mention it. I forgot to ask."

"Gaynor got any ideas about who could have done it?"

"One. Carol. He says Frank must have seen her at the apartment last night and held out hoping for a pay-off." He paused while he considered telling Carter about the check, decided not to.

Carter nodded absently, as though such information was unimportant at the moment. When he finally continued there was a connotation of some unspoken horror in his tone.

"Jesus, that's sure rough about Quinn!" he said slowly. "I didn't know him well like you did, but he seemed like a pretty decent guy."

"He was."

Fenner started toward his car, wanting to

be alone so he could grieve a little in private for his friend. Carter, keeping pace, was talking again and Fenner had to concentrate to follow his comments.

"I heard he was a comer years ago. A fine firm to work for, a bright future ahead until he had some personal trouble he couldn't handle. Was it booze or his wife?"

"Both," Fenner said, not wanting to think about it. "I don't know which came first."

They took a few steps in silence until Carter took his arm and pulled him to a stop. A new intentness was working in the reporter's eyes and his brows were knotted, as though he had just now accepted the theory Fenner had passed along from Sergeant Gaynor.

"You think he did see Carol? Quinn?" Then, answering himself, he said: "Suppose he saw a way to make a score and hinted at a settlement for his silence. But even then where would she get a gun in the middle of the night? Why shoot him when she could pay off and never miss the dough? I don't buy it." He paused again, the frown biting deeper. "The thing that bugs me is, where the hell is she?"

"Frank could have seen something else," Fenner said irritably, tired of such speculation.

"Like what?"

"Who the hell can say what he saw? Maybe some character we don't even know about. A guy like Browning had to make enemies. Plenty of them. Who knows? Maybe Frank lied about the time schedule he gave me; you heard it."

"You mean Grayson and Hubbard? Yeah," Carter added thoughtfully. "I guess you could work up some kind of motive . . . Look, Jack. I know how you must feel about Frank Quinn. You must have liked him; you were sort of business roommates. Let me buy you a drink. You look as if you could use one. Come on. Consider it medicinal."

"Not now, Sam. Thanks just the same."

"How about lunch then? It's not a good time to be alone."

Fenner did not know Carter well except by reputation from various sources, chiefly Carol Browning and Kent Murdock, but he was strangely touched by this genuine concern for his feelings. He said so as he released his arm.

"I appreciate it, Sam. I really do. But I ought to get back. Somebody's got to get in touch with Frank's wife; I think he was still married. I seem to remember that there's a brother around somewhere. He may have some addresses in his desk. I have to find out what Homicide is doing about it and when the examiner can release the body."

He managed a light and friendly punch on the other's shoulder. "Some other time. And, oh, tell Murdock about this when you get back, will you? Say I'll call him later. I think he'd like to know."

Carter leaned in the open window opposite the driver's seat as Fenner got behind the wheel and Fenner sensed the change in expression. No wrinkled brow now, a speculative distance in the intelligent amber eyes.

"Just one thing more," he said. "I seem to have a hazy sort of hunch. You ever get them?"

"Hunches?" It was Fenner's turn to squint. "Now and then."

A thin smile showed beneath the

mustache. "All good reporters get them once in a while. You learn to play along with them if you're any good."

Fenner sighed patiently. "All right, Sam, what does this one say?"

"That you've been in touch with Carol since she disappeared from Ufford. That you might even have seen her, or maybe you just know where she can be found."

The accuracy of the reporter's guess shocked Fenner and he wondered if his reaction showed. He concentrated on making his reply convincing and his voice held a note of ridicule.

"Some hunch, Sam. I heard you were a gambling man."

"Sometimes. In my own quiet way."

Fenner turned the ignition key. "Then don't bet on this one. The odds are prohibitive. You ought to know that . . . Be sure and tell Murdock, hunh?"

13

It was after 1:30 when Jack Fenner returned to his office. The door was locked, the customary procedure when Alice Maxwell went out for lunch. The telephone, he knew, would have been switched to the answering-service line and he went first to his private office to see if there were any messages. Finding none he rang the answering service.

"Jack Fenner," he said. "Anything for me?"

"Just one call, Mr. Fenner. About a half hour ago, but the party wouldn't leave her name."

"A woman?"

"Yes. She said she'd call later."

Fenner hung up and got rid of his topcoat and Shetland jacket. He loosened his tie and the top button of his blue Oxford shirt, then slouched in his upholstered desk chair, depressed and still shaken by the morning's events.

He got a cigarette going, not knowing that he did so. He swiveled the chair and stared sightlessly out the window at the office building across the way, noting the movement of the clerks and stenographers behind other windows. Gradually the state of utter ennui began to pass and he thought first of the bottom drawer of his desk where he kept a bottle of good bourbon. This reminded him of the drink Sam Carter offered and he realized he needed it now. Somehow this thought triggered another and he was suddenly aware that he was hungry. The word set up a silent mental argument. Was he hungry, or just empty? Toying with the idea for another minute or so, he grunted softly and reached for the telephone, dialing a delicatessen halfway down the side street. When he had an answer he asked for Eddie.

"Jack Fenner, Eddie."

"Yes, Mr. Fenner, and how are you today?"

"You got any Swiss cheese?"

"The best."

"With ham and rye bread. A little lettuce, mayonnaise *and* mustard."

"Right. Coffee?"

"Black and don't fill the container until you're going out the door."

"Hot, hunh?" Eddie said. "I gotcha, Mr. Fenner."

Having made this first important decision, Fenner promptly made another and reached for the bourbon bottle. There was a small table at the window end of the desk made of veneered walnut and two inches lower than the desk top. It held a portable electric typewriter that he sometimes used nights when he was alone and wanted to get some thoughts on paper.

There was also a gray metal tray, a pint-sized carafe to match, and two glasses. The carafe, he knew, would have been filled with cold water from the electric cooler in the outer office. The glasses were sparkking as always because Alice Maxwell kept a dish towel, changed once a week, and a supply of soap powder in her desk.

Now he poured an inch and a half of whisky, added water, and took a large swallow, feeling its warmth in his gullet until the whisky began its work on his stomach tissues. He went over to open his office door so he could know when Eddie came with the sandwich. This happened two swallows later, and when he had approved of the sandwich and felt the coffee container, he paid the check and added a half dollar . . .

It was after two when Alice Maxwell came back and by that time Fenner's desk had been cleaned of the luncheon debris, the whisky was back in its drawer, and the decision made as to how he was going to break the news to the girl. He waited until she had examined her face and found it satisfactory and then asked her to come in.

"Sit down, Alice, please." He waited until she had settled herself, feeling her expectant and puzzled brown eyes upon him. Then, though he had wrestled with the problem in an effort to find some easier way, he was left with no alternative but to come right out and tell her. "I've got some bad news."

"About Mrs. Browning?" she asked,

voice hushed but alert.

He shook his head. "Frank Quinn."

"Oh, dear. Something happened to him?"

"He's dead, Alice." He watched the shocked young face crumble, the sudden pallor as the eyes began to fill. "It happened last night," he said and went on quickly, determined to get it over and sticking to the essential facts.

He felt lousy all over again when he finished, and he wanted very much to pull her to her feet and take her in his arms, for she had made no sound, no comment, as she bowed her head and the tears came silently and uncontrolled.

"Do you want a drink, Alice?" he said finally, desperate now for some way to ease the emotional shock.

She shook her head and sniffed loudly. She looked up finally, the cheeks tear-stained and still pale.

"He was such a nice man," she said and started looking in her lap, apparently for the handkerchief that wasn't there. Fenner gave her the one in the breast pocket of his jacket and she blew her nose and began to dab at the wet cheeks.

"I'm all right now," she said, and tried to smile.

The effort that smile took moved Fenner and he looked away as he went on matter-of-factly to explain what Quinn had been doing for him the night before.

"It looks as if Frank made a bad mistake," he said as he finished. "He must have seen the killer and for some reason kept that knowledge to himself . . . Now, have you heard from Mrs. Browning this morning?" he asked to change the subject. "I think she called when we were out," he added when she shook her head.

"The answering service said a woman phoned but wouldn't leave her name. Oh, yeah, do you know if Mrs. Browning went out last night at any time?"

"If she did I didn't hear her."

"Did you know Kent Murdock and I came there last night?"

"She told me this morning."

"You didn't hear us?"

"No."

He manufactured a grin for her. "I guess you sleep pretty good."

"Like a top," she said, "whatever that

means." And now he thought he saw a glimmer of a smile in her eyes.

"If anyone came to your place after that you probably wouldn't know about it."

"I didn't hear anyone, if that's what you mean."

"Okay. Now here is what I'd like you to do. The chances are Mrs. Browning will phone again. If she does I'm not in, even if I am, understand?"

She nodded, the pert face very serious now.

"You don't know where I am, or where to reach me."

"What do I tell her?"

"Tell her I called in to say there has been some developments that I want to check out before I talk to her and that I'll be out to see her when I can; that she's to stay put until I get in touch."

He thought back over what he had said. He wanted to see Carol Browning badly, but he didn't want to talk to her over the phone. There were questions that had to be answered, but there were other things he wanted to do first. When he did see her he wanted to have all the information he could get. He was about to dismiss Alice when he remembered one more vital point.

"Whatever you do, don't tell her about Frank Quinn. You don't know anything. You don't even know he was working for me. All you know is that he hasn't been in today. I doubt if she'll mention him, but I don't want her to know what happened until I can tell her personally."

He stood up with her and she gave him back his handkerchief. "You could do one more thing. I think Frank still had a wife, somewhere in the Southwest I think. There's also a brother in upstate New York, maybe Buffalo. We've no legal right to touch his things. I don't know who has, but someone will be around. Just take a quick look through his desk right now before the police get here. See if you can find an address book or anything that might tell us how to get in touch with the brother or wife..."

Jack Fenner knew the Walker House as a moderatly priced hostelry, no longer quite as fashionable but properly run, the clerks

191

trained to to accept drunks and hookers who wanted to register without luggage. It still had a reputation for good food in the paneled grill room, its most famous creation a well-known roll that had been named after this culinary achievement.

The desk clerk, acting on his request, gave him the room number and he went to the house phones. Again he was lucky to find his man in.

"Mr. Grayson?" he said, "I'm Jack Fenner. You don't know me but I'm a friend of your stepsister. I'm a private investigator and I've done quite a bit of work for her in the past. I'd like to talk to you if you can give me a few minutes."

"Sure, Mr. Fenner," Grayson said without hesitation. "Come on up. Nine-twelve."

Room 912 was but a few steps down the hall from the elevators. His knock was answered almost immediately by a big, genial-looking man, and it seemed at once obvious from his coloring and features that he could hardly be a blood relation to Carol Browning.

His hair was black and straight, worn a

bit long but not yet curling over the collar of his cashmere jacket. The eyes were black and lively, the brows thick and nearly meeting above the bridge of his nose. He had a strong, rugged-looking jaw and a quick, wide smile too, but Fenner was not aware of this until later.

"Mr. Fenner?" he said. "Come in. I was about to have a small snort. Will you join me?"

It occurred to Fenner that he was doing well in the free-drink department that day: Mona Vail, the invitation from Sam Carter, and now this.

"Not right now, thanks. You go ahead."

"I think I will. Sit down anywhere."

Aside from the double bed there was not much "anywhere" to be found—a club chair drably covered, two matching straight-backed chairs. Fenner took the one by the table desk and watched his host pour Scotch and water over ice cubes whose sharp edges suggested they had been recently ordered.

Grayson said: "Sure now?" and drank thirstily when Fenner again declined. "First today. In my racket you learn to lay off the stuff at noon." He eased into the club chair. "You said over the phone that you were a friend of Carol's. Maybe you can clue me in as to where in hell she's been hiding. How did you know where to find me?" he added in his nonstop fashion. "I've only been in town three or four days."

"They told me at police headquarters. A sergeant named Joe Gaynor said you'd been in this morning."

"Oh," he said, sobering as a small frown showed. "You know about that."

"Gaynor said you read about the Browning murder in the paper and came in to—"

"That's right. I thought maybe they knew where my stepsister was, but all they could tell me was that she was missing. I got the impression that they're thinking she may have shot him, which is a lot of pure unadulterated crap . . . Do *you* know where she is?"

Fenner shook his head, preferring the silent lie to the spoken word.

"You say you did some work for her?"

"Right."

"Yeah." Grayson took another swallow

and stared into his glass, black eyes full of gloom. "I remember now. She mentioned in one of her letters that she had a private detective working for her. That was you, hunh? And I got the idea from things she said that she had more divorce evidence than she could possibly use. That means you must have known that bastard husband of hers pretty well."

"I was working for him when he was killed."

"You what?"

"He hired me about two hours or so before he was found."

Grayson seemed confused by the unexpected revelation. He finished his drink, jiggled the ice cubes, scowled at them, seemed undecided about another drink, finally put the empty glass on the window sill.

"Well, that's a switch. What the hell did *he* want?"

"The same thing you did. To find her."

"She just up and disappeared?"

"There's a state mental hospital at a place called Ufford thirty or forty miles west of the city. Browning had your stepsister committed there about two weeks ago."

For a second or two Grayson just stared, his eyes shocked, incredulous, and bright with anger.

"A state institution for Christ's sake! Why the miserable sonofabitch. She could have paid her way in any private place in the country. For as long as she wanted. What's the rest of it?"

Fenner went over the familiar story, his angular face impassive, his voice steady and unaccented as he recounted the facts as he knew them.

"Do you think this Browning bastard was telling the truth, that she was out of her skull? Who's this doctor who signed the papers? Garic?"

"He seems to be a reputable man. Apparently Browning insisted and as the husband he could call the shots."

"And she just walked off yesterday, hunh? Well, good for her . . . So he came to you and said find her, and I guess you went down to her apartment and parked there hoping she'd show up sometime."

"I did a little more than that. On the off

chance that she might have holed up in her apartment, I went up to have a look. When I walked in, Browning was there on the floor with two slugs in him."

"You're the guy that found him? Well, I'll be damned."

He chewed on this new information while things happened behind his eyes and then came up with a good question.

"How did you get in?"

Fenner, long aware that one lie usually compounds another said: "The door was unlocked."

"Not when I tried it."

"This was later. Around 7:30."

"And this morning you went to police headquarters? This sergeant, whatever his name is—he a friend of yours?"

"Yes."

"He told you about my coming in, and why?"

"Right."

"I'd called Carol's number maybe a half dozen times in the past couple of days, went up there yesterday afternoon. I put away a few drinks later, and I was getting burned by then, so I tried again last night. This time

I thought I saw a lighted window on her floor so I went up and buzzed awhile, and knocked, tried the door. The light bothered me until I realized later when I was out on the street that I'd been wrong about it. I thought about getting the janitor to open up but I didn't know where the hell to find him . . . Who else the cops got on their suspect list?"

"Her ex-husband for one. He apparently went there for the same reason you did, with the same result."

"I met him. Quite a while back. At the wedding actually. Hubbard. Isn't that his name? Seemed like a nice guy; don't know why Carol would divorce him; never did know."

"Her uncle was there too," Fenner said, and explained how Lamont Grayson had walked in on him.

Barry Grayson's comment was explosive and pungent. "That penny-pinching bastard. But not for long, not for long." He had been glaring across the room, black eyes brooding; now he turned them on Fenner. "You know about the Grayson trust?"

"In a general way. I understand Tuesday, the fifteenth, is settlement day."

Grayson grunted, his gaze quizzical as he considered the statement. "You seem to know quite a lot about Carol and her affairs."

"I did a lot of work for her. She was my star client for a while. Once I got digging on Browning and his activities she seemed to get the itch about others around her."

"Like who?"

"Hubbard, her uncle and his mistress, a reporter friend of hers named Sam Carter."

"Not me?" Grayson's smile showed for the first time. When it broadened, Fenner decided it had much to recommend it.

"Not you," he said, his approval of this man expanding. "All I know about you is the few things Carol told me from time to time."

"Like what?"

"Well, that you were left fifty grand and twenty percent of the estate, that you grabbed the fifty and took off for Europe. Wasn't it Switzerland and some hotel school?"

"At first. I never was much of a student

199

but I squeezed through with an A.B., which prepared me for nothing. I'd spent a lot of time in night clubs and I guess I figured, What the hell, why not learn how to run one of your own?"

This time when he glanced at the empty glass he could no longer resist. He stepped over to make a fresh drink, remembered his manners, and repeated his original invitation. This time Fenner accepted.

"Thanks," he said, "if it's not too much trouble. Make it the same as yours."

"It was just a thought at first," Grayson said, handing Fenner his glass, "but later I ran into this guy from Germany who had the same idea so we took off for the south of France, working other places while we looked around for some joint we could buy into. What we'd learned in Switzerland was enough to get us jobs as waiters and we kept our ears open—I tended bar awhile—and we kept hearing about this place in Spain. Torremolinos. You know it?

"Booming," he said when Fenner shook his head. "You wouldn't believe it. From a little Spanish fishing village to a jerry-built Miami Beach. Property values out of sight.

Anyway, I had most of my inheritance and Gunnar had some money, so we bought into a little place and settled in to make our fortune. We hung in there pretty good for a couple of years, losing a little each month until we realized we'd found a slow way of going broke. Neither of us knew much Spanish in the beginning, so it wasn't too hard for bartenders to clip us in small but continuing ways, for the chef to set up petty deals with the local suppliers.

"Along about that time I began hearing good things about Barbados and pretty soon I had the itch to move out of Torremolinos and Gunnar was fed up too; also we were getting low on funds. So we sold our interest for what we could get and shook hands. Gunnar wanted to have another go at the south of France and I flew to Barbados to have a look."

Fenner shifted his buttocks in the hard wooden seat and tried a new position, content to let the other ramble on as he did his own private thinking.

"How did that work out?" he asked, knowing they would eventually get to Denver.

"It didn't. Lovely place, though. Best climate in the world, especially in winter. I spent a couple of weeks there nosing around trying to get a rough history of the night club and restaurant business there. Hilton and Holiday were building then not far from the center of Bridgetown, and the Platinum Coast on the leeward side was mostly society, British and American, aging jet-setters and one-time movie stars, minor diplomats, most with houses, or guests of houses. The dinner-party-type crowd who entertained at home.

"It wasn't too long before I found out the only guy who ever ran a successful night club over a period of years was an American — Frank Morgan — from Connecticut. He battled the whole damn British establishment to a standstill; I say British because that's what most of them were; remittance-men-types with a little backing. They'd open some spot with a big fanfare and newspaper ads, flourish for a few months, and fade away. Morgan hung in there for thirty years or so and got a proper offer a few years back and sold out to a guy who came over from Venezuela with big ideas and no savvy. When he blew the whole bit, Morgan made apartments out of the club and still lives on the island eight or nine months of the year . . . Hey!"

His smile reappeared suddenly as he realized how much he had been talking. "This is getting a little monotonous, isn't it?"

Fenner grinned back at him. "I'm waiting for the Denver part."

"Okay. It won't be long now. Anyway, I figured the setup looked too tough for a guy with diminishing capital so, big brain that I am, I said let's go to some undeveloped island, Barry boy, and grow with the tourist trade. Trinidad was out. Tobago, with real fine beaches, was too quiet, but even there Hilton was making plans for a new hotel. Grenada, also with marvelous beaches, was getting built up, with Holiday starting construction of another inn.

"I finally settled on St. Vincent. By then they had an airstrip—before that you got in twice weekly on a Grumman Goose—and a small but exclusive place on a little island a couple of hundred yards offshore. Some say the Beatles started it, but you couldn't prove it by me. So I finally took a six-month option on a twelve-room inn across from this Young's Island."

He laughed out loud, a cheerful, spontaneous sound. "Six months was all I needed, believe me. I decided I couldn't wait to grow up with the tourist trade because it was altogether too damn slow in coming and I could see slow starvation standing in the wings.

"The only good to come out of it was this fellow who spent a week with me. He'd been around and he tipped me off to this Denver possibility." He grinned again. "Last lap," he said.

"By that time I knew a little more than the guy who started out in Torremolinos and I had ten grand left. I had some correspondence with the owner, and a couple of overseas calls, and I learned that I could get a small piece of this spot for thirty G's if I got in there and managed the show. It looked so good I wrote dear Lamont, explaining the situation and asking for an advance on my twenty percent. He turned me down flat, so I wrote Carol. Luckily she was a little flush at the time. She gave me twenty and wouldn't even take my note, which shows what kind of a kid she is. Said she knew I owed it, and I knew, and pay off when I could. A month or so ago I got the chance to gain control for another fifty. One month, mind you, before I get my share, but old Pinchpenny still wouldn't give me the advance. So I'm here waiting for the fifteenth. After that I should be all set. I've got a year's option to buy the joint, which I will, because I've worked it into one of the best places in the city to eat, and later hear some of the finest Dixie being played today. Period. End of confession."

Fenner stood up and stretched. The fact that he had spent a lot of time here listening to background information that seemed relatively unimportant did not bother him. He had spent many such unproductive hours during his career. It was a necessary part of the job because one could never tell when just one innocuous sentence could lead to more pertinent information. Now he asked Grayson if he could use the phone, and when he got the nod he dialed the *Courier* number and asked for the studio.

When Ken Murdock answered he said: "If you'll eat an early dinner with me, I'll pick up the check."

"I like the check part, buy why early?"

"There are some things I want to do this evening. I've got time now, if you have . . . you heard about Frank Quinn?"

"Sam Carter told me."

"Don't you want to know more?"

"I guess I do at that. Give me a half hour?"

"You got it. I can spend that much time drinking and still have a couple with you. Lobster?"

"I hear you."

"Terroni's in a half hour."

He hung up, shook hands with Barry Grayson, thanked him for his time.

"I guess you're still trying to find Carol?" Grayson said.

"That's right," Fenner said, the lie coming easily.

"Well, if you do, will you please ask her to give me a ring?" Fenner said he would.

14

Terroni's had little style because it was too well lighted and its plain, white-topped tables marched in orderly rows with no refinements like booths and banquettes done in imitation leather. You ate right out in the open—the best that could be hoped for was a wall table—and if that was distasteful, you didn't come. A long bar on the left served hot meat sandwiches for those in a hurry at lunchtime, but its reputation was based on providing the best seafood dishes in the city.

Fenner, at the bar, was still on his first martini on the rocks when Kent Murdock arrived, and because it was early they had no trouble getting a wall table. Fenner brought his unfinished drink and when the waiter came with water and silver, Murdock ordered a duplicate. When it came he told the waiter to bring two more in ten minutes.

"Okay," he said, lifting his glass in the manner of a toast, "this one's for Frank Quinn, the poor little guy. A thing like that makes you kind of sick, doesn't it? Goes for a ride with someone and winds up dead. Never had a chance, did he?"

Fenner didn't want to think about it, but because he had some things to say he could not avoid the subject no matter how distasteful. He kept waiting for the martini to warm him and said: "How much did Carter tell you?"

"He said Quinn apparently had both hands on the wheel when whoever it was stuck the gun in his ribs and squeezed twice. Sometime around midnight. Carter said he talked to you, said you more or less agreed that Quinn had to have seen someone else last night and kept it to himself, probably expecting some pay-off for his silence."

Fenner nodded, angular face morose and distance in his gaze. "Either that or he lied about the time those three callers went into the building."

"Carter doesn't know who our hippie was?"

"Nobody knows. But there's something

else I can tell you that I couldn't tell Carter," he said and spoke of the check for twenty thousand Sergeant Gaynor had found on the body.

He watched Murdock lean slowly forward, forearms brushing the silver aside, the dark eyes narrowing in shocked disbelief. He made an obvious effort to tighten the slackness in his jaw before he could reply.

"Jesus, Jack!" he said, his voice full of awe. "A twenty thousand payoff? And it was Carol's check?"

"A blank check form, but I'm pretty sure it was her signature."

"But how in God's name did he get to her? He didn't know that hippie he saw was Carol."

"Oh yes he did," Fenner said, his self-disgust showing in his voice. "I had a private word with him last night when you moved off after you and Carter had heard his report. I told him who that hippie was — probably one of my greatest all-time mistakes, damn it to hell — because I wanted to impress on him the importance of pinning down the exact time he saw this hippie so we'd know whether she came out of the building before Browning got there or after. If you can stand it without belting me, I also told him Carol was staying with Alice Maxwell until we could find out what the score was."

He took an open-mouthed breath, unable quite to disguise the tremendous distaste he felt, let it out noisily with an air of hopeless resignation.

"So there you have it," he said bitterly. "Old Jack Fenner, the super-sleuth, the cagey one. Goddammit! Frank Quinn might be alive if I'd kept my big mouth shut."

Murdock's reply was at once sympathetic. "That's nothing but wild conjecture and you know it. Frank had to have gone to see Carol after we left, right? So suppose he did hit her for a big pay-off. She gave it to him. Why not? She could afford it."

"She could have conned him into taking her for a ride easily enough," Fenner argued half-heartedly. "Alice says she didn't even hear us. She certainly didn't hear Frank or she'd have said so."

"Using whose gun? Carol, I mean. And

then leaving the check after she killed him? Come on, Jackson, talk sense."

"I said the same thing to Joe Gaynor when he showed me the check," Fenner said, still unconvinced, "and he said who could say a woman wouldn't panic. In a closed car those two shots probably would sound like a stick of dynamite. It could scare the hell out of her. She'd probably think the sound could be heard four blocks away. The only thing in her mind would be to get the hell away from there before someone grabbed her with the gun in her hand."

Murdock seemed ready to continue the argument when something changed his mind. Troubled lights were working on his dark eyes and worry lines were visible in his lean, strong face as he struggled with his problem.

"All right," he said. "Let me ask you a question. Do you think," he added, hesitating now as though afraid to finish the sentence, "that she could have killed him?"

"Skip what I think. Look at the facts." Fenner ticked them off, starting with the little finger. "She got the key from the super and admits she went there. She had more motive than a lot of women who have killed their husbands. There is no way of pinning down the time she was there. I mean, there's a gap in the story she told us at your place about how long it took to walk there, how long she stood getting up her nerve after she got that key."

He ticked off his last finger. "And remember how evasive Quinn was in committing himself about when he saw our hippie?" He started to reach for a cigarette and his willpower stopped him. "So let me ask *you* a question and it comes down to this: do you believe — can you believe — her or not?"

Murdock ducked that one and digressed. "Have you talked to her today?"

"No."

"Why the hell not?"

"After the thing with Quinn I was afraid to."

"Afraid?"

"All right. Let's just say I wasn't ready for her. There were other things I wanted to find out."

"Like what?"

"I wanted to talk to this Barry Grayson, get a chance to size him up. I wanted to talk to Alan Hubbard, but he'll have to wait until tomorrow. When I leave here I want to do some checking on Mr. Lamont Grayson. Because I've been thinking about George Browning's income and the way he lived. When Carol kicked him out she cut off his charge accounts and credit; she still gave him a grand a month for nuisance money. He lived at the University Club, but he had this pad in that building right next to her apartment.

"He was sleeping now and then with Grayson's private secretary and who the hell can say what a woman will tell a man when she's in bed and happy and maybe thinking he'll marry her after he gets divorced. Old Grayson has been handling that two- or three-million-buck trust fund for a long time. He could have been manipulating a bit here and there. Some of it would have to show on some sort of record, and who'd know better what the score was than a trusted private secretary?" He stopped abruptly, seeing his friend's dark scowl. "What's the matter?"

"I'm trying to keep up. You think maybe Grayson's been dipping into those funds. He has to turn them over next week; he's got to know there's going to be a thorough and intensive audit of his accounts."

"So I'm grabbing at straws. What else is there? I'm going to see Carol later and lay it all on the line. Before I do I'm going to have a look at Browning's little love nest and see if I can find anything that can help. What have I got to lose?"

"Your license if you get caught," Murdock said dryly. "You're skating on pretty thin ice as it is."

"So are you."

"Yours is thinner. Carol's going to have to talk to the police sooner or later. If they get the idea that we've been holding out, the D.A. may give me a hard time but I'll still have a job. She isn't even your client. Dammit, you haven't got a client."

"Browning."

"A dead man."

"He's still a client."

"She's going to have to turn herself in," Murdock argued.

"I know."

"When?"

"I thought tomorrow morning. It can wait one more night and I've got some things to say to her first . . . Look, let's eat before I get too scared. Another drink first?"

"I'm content." Murdock tapped the menu. "You're paying for it, you order."

Fenner didn't need a menu. He looked across at his friend, saw the familiar small grin that was reflected openly in the dark, well-spaced eyes and somehow that look made him feel immeasurably better. "Oysters?"

"A half-dozen Cotuits, if you please sir."

"Lobster?"

"A pound and a quarter to a half; no larger."

"Salad?"

"With oil and vinegar."

Fenner beckoned to the waiter, concurring in every respect with Murdock's choice except for the salad dressing. "One oil and vinegar," he said. "One French."

Terroni had built his reputation for his lobsters not by half-cooking them beforehand and then slapping them under a broiler when ordered to save time. You ordered and they were taken out of their salt-water tank and split live before broiling. This took twenty minutes or so, but most customers thought the result well worth the time.

Now the two old friends sipped the last of their drinks, silent with their thoughts for several minutes before Murdock went back to the things that still bothered him.

"You're willing to take a chance busting into this hideout of Browning's without really knowing what you're after?"

"I don't think it will be too much of a chance. I'm a very clever lock-picker."

"Breaking and entering if you slip up."

"No. Illegal entry."

"If there's anything there that might help, don't you think the police would have turned it up?"

"I'm betting the police don't even know about the place. Browning rented it under another name. When they go through his things at his University Club room they could get a lead to it, but so what? If they've cleaned out his secret pad all I've wasted is a little of my time. And who knows, maybe lightning will strike."

They both knew how to demolish and enjoy a broiled lobster and because of their concentrated endeavors nothing was said until they had used the necessary post-lobster fingerbowls. Only when the coffee came and Fenner's offer of a brandy was refused did they have time for further serious discussion and that was brief.

It happened when Fenner reached for the check. As he did so Murdock put a firm hand on Fenner's forearm, not to take the check away but as a gesture of concerned friendship.

"Just watch yourself, Jackson. I mean, when you see Carol, and whether or not you find anything at Browning's place that helps. Make her understand that if she blows this caper for us we'll be boxed in good, you especially, with no standing with the police and your license on the line. I don't think she should even tell Lamont Grayson where she's been or how she got there, assuming she wants him to represent her."

Fenner nodded as Murdock released his arm. "From what we know," Murdock added, "there's no way I can see how she could kill Frank Quinn unless she sneaked out of the Maxwell girl's place last night, but there's still the Browning murder."

He leaned back as Fenner put a bill on the check and this time the small grin came.

"Phone me before you call it a night. I just hope you don't have to do it from some precinct house . . ."

Jack Fenner had a bit of luck when he was ready to enter the seven-story apartment building where George Browning had his two-and-a-half-room love nest. He had left his car well down the street and it was his intention to wait near some car parked close to the entrance where he could linger until he saw some tenant coming through the vestibule. The glass door made this practical and he intended to time his approach from outside so that he could get the door before it closed.

As it happened he was walking four or five steps behind an elderly couple, paying them no attention until he saw them turn in just in front of him. The man had his key in hand and Fenner lagged a bit until the door was unlocked and simply followed them in with a smile and a "Thank you" as the man politely held the door for him.

They went to one of the automatic elevators and the man said, "Six for us," and punched the proper button. Fenner said, "Four, please."

When he got out he said good night, moved to the fire door, and went down to the floor below. He knew the apartment he wanted was at the front and all he asked now was that the corridor stay empty another minute. He could have forced the ordinary lock with a celluloid strip, but the gadget he carried for just such occasions would look better in case someone stepped into the hall as he worked at the keyhold.

This took him about eight seconds and so intent was he on the task that he stepped into a darkened room without the slightest premonition that anything was wrong. There may have been a long instant as he swung the door behind him and groped for a light switch, a moment of blackness during which he sensed that he was not alone. Then the moment was gone and the focused beam of a flashlight hit him smack in the eyes. At

219

the same time a gruff voice, obviously distorted but with a note of authority said:

"Stand still!"

Fenner froze, one foot in front of the other while his heart flopped back in place, blinking against the sudden brightness and seeing nothing at all until the muzzle of a gun was projected purposely into the cone of light.

"See the gun?"

"I see it."

"It can go off if you try anything."

What's to try?" Fenner said, speaking past the dryness in his throat and trying to find something familiar in the voice. He watched the light move back a few feet and slowly start to circle before it flicked sideways in a signal of its own and the voice ordered:

"Over by the wall next to the TV."

Fenner did not turn his back but moved crablike and with deliberate slowness so he could watch the light. For by now his eyes had adjusted somewhat and he got a glimpse of the hand holding the gun. He knew how difficult it would be for the man to hold it just far enough into the beam to be seen and not far enough to give anything away. By the time he reached for the wall with one hand he was able to make out the edge of a dark coat sleeve. A half inch of French shirt cuff showed briefly and he got a glint of yellow, suggesting gold cuff links.

"Face it. Hands flat. Legs back now. Spread them and lean hard."

Fenner knew what was wanted. He had issued the same order in the past. Since he had no intention of jumping the gun in that position he simply waited, feeling the other's presence move close as the light beam plastered his shadow against the wall.

One hand came as expected, patting hips, beltline, reaching carefully under his extended arms to feel his chest, first on one side and then on the other as his wallet was removed and the light seemed to back up slightly.

"Just hold it there and stay healthy!" the voice said.

"I'm holding it," Fenner said, pleased that his voice sounded so casual and indifferent.

For that first quick thrust of fear had long since evaporated and there was no tremor in his arms or legs as his mind went coldly about its business of assessing the situation. There was no thought now of a bullet in his back, since if the object was murder it would have already been carried out. Common sense told him that the intruder's chief objective would be to get away unseen and he waited patiently for the next move, hearing the other's grunt.

"A private detective? Where's your gun?"

"What gun?"

"I thought they all carried one."

"Only in television. In television they carry guns and shoot the bad guys with no questions asked; no inquiries, no hearings, no grand jury investigations. The whole thing is a breeze. In real life if a P.I. shoots anyone he's in trouble up to here."

He kept peering back beneath his armpit hoping for some revealing clue that might help him identify the man. To gain time he kept talking.

"A private dick has no more right to use a gun than any citizen who happens to have a permit to carry one. Either way the guy'll find himself in more trouble than he can handle, which makes me wonder if you have a permit to have that piece you're holding on me.

"Just don't believe what you see on TV," he added, warming to his subject. "It's mostly fiction or fantasy and don't blame the writers. The producer has a formula and a writer better put in the proper ingredients. You know how it goes. The shoot-out at the end, generally at the top of a tower or a scaffold or a birdge. Because it's essential that the bad guy try to get away by climbing high so the viewer can see a body in some spectacular fall, right? And the P.D. heroes tuck their guns in their belts—fade out. If you think at all, you're supposed to assume they'll be exonerated if and when, at some later date, there is an inquiry—"

"Shut up!"'

The quick, hard thrust of the gun made Fenner flinch and obey. He heard his wallet thud to the carpet near one foot.

"Pick it up. Nice and easy. Now back toward me."

Fenner straightened after he had retrieved the wallet. He replaced it and shook his coat sleeves down. He started to back up, a foot at a time.

"A little more to your left."

The light beam was retreating now, circling slightly to the right.

Fenner kept backing, inches at a time now, seeing the features of the room reveal themselves in front of him. He had been listening very carefully to the unseen voice but it remained annoyingly constant, the hoarse gruffs accents distorted but remarkably in key.

He was nearly across the room, the light on his right now, when he heard a door open. He stopped, certain that it was not the hall door. The voice told him to keep moving. Finally it said:

"Okay, now turn around, all the way."

When Fenner did so he was directly in front of an open closet just inside the outer door. Now, aware what the other wanted and not waiting for the next command, he stepped inside.

"Good man. All the way now." The light was close again and the muzzle of the gun dug lightly into his spine. "Flat against the wall."

Fenner pushed a coat out of the way and

the voice said: "I'm going to shut that door and lock it. You jump me before I turn the key and the gun goes off."

The door closed and blackness came. Fenner, having had no intention of making his move until it was safe, heard the lock click. He turned then to face it, listening intently until he heard the outer door open and close.

He hit the panel then with a lowered shoulder but that first attempt told him that the space was too cramped to get sufficient momentum. The same shallowness helped him when he put his back against the wall, got one foot flat against the door with knee bent. When he had the other in place he was properly jacknifed and he put all he had into his back and thigh muscles.

The panel cracked and he grunted and strained and the flimsy lock tore loose. His legs shot forward and he came down hard on his rump.

Not bothering with the lights or even considering the hall door he went at once to the two front windows. One, with an air-conditioning unit was sealed, but the other came up at his tug and he leaned out to see a man cross the sidewalk and step into the street.

He was hoping this was his man, that he would glance up just once to reveal his face. When the other seemed intent on flagging the next taxi, he cataloged what he was able to see. Foreshortened as the angle was, he could only guess that the man was taller than most, with a dark coat and hat and no other revealing features.

Then he was stepping farther into the street and a taxi swooped to a stop just ahead. The door opened and the man ducked and disappeared as the cab accelerated. The high angle made identification of the license plate impossible and when he closed the window he turned on the overhead light and looked at his watch.

Seven fifty-two. A Yellow-and-Black hack. Now if this happened to be a driver who was conscientious about keeping his trip sheet in proper order, the odds on locating him tomorrow should be good.

15

With the light on and his eyes busy, Fenner had his first good look at the room and he realized then that it had been searched. He could not be sure how thoroughly, but he did not stop to wonder then, continuing instead to the bedroom. When he found nothing out of order, he was ready to believe that either the intruder had been interrupted before he could get to the bedroom or that he had already found what he wanted when Fenner walked in.

Now, hoping this would be the case, he left the bedroom and inspected the outer room more carefully. It had the look of an apartment that had been rented furnished, since what pieces there were had little taste. The Lawson sofa had a used and battered look. The slipcovers on the two easy chairs badly needed dry cleaning; the end tables were spotted and scarred by cigarettes left too long on the edges, the kneehole desk was thinly veneered and peeling slightly at one corner. Thin, washed-out rugs, an imitation Boston rocker, and two straight-backed chairs. That was all except for the lamps and the portable TV set on a standard.

The drawers of the tables were pulled partway out; so were two of the desk drawers. The sofa cushions had been removed and were still piled on top of each other; the cushions of the easy chairs were askew and one lampshade was crooked.

Without much hope of finding anything worthwhile, Fenner went first to the desk and sat in its chair. As he examined the drawers one by one he saw that they were more cluttered than he had expected. There was no personal correspondence, but there were paper and envelopes, bills, mail-order catalogs, discarded pens and pencils, clips, rubber bands, and some mail-order ciculars from a pornographic photographer. Then far back in the center drawer he found a checkbook on the Park Street Bank.

Wondering why it was here instead of Browning's room in the University Club, he glanced at the stubs. He saw that each one was made out to cash and in the same amount. Digging deeper among the debris he found a few bank statements secured by a rubber band. The canceled checks, only one to a statement, matched the stubs and he began to see why this particular checkbook and the canceled checks might be something Browning had not wanted to leave in his other room where daily maid service and prying eyes might find them.

His unexpected discovery puzzled him only briefly, and his mind moved on as his imagination took over. His first thought, prompted by the fact that the checks were drawn in the same amount—five hundred dollars—and all made out to cash, suggested George Browning had been paying someone blackmail. The thought found substance when he turned the checks over and saw Browning's endorsement.

This further suggested that the blackmailer was cagey enough to demand his payments in cash so there would be no record of his signature.

The dates were all the first or second of the month. There was no way of telling how long Browning had been paying since there were only four checks and four matching stubs in the new-looking checkbook. Apparently this account had been used for but one purpose. To confirm the hunch he remembered the check for a retainer Browning had given him the evening before. He took it from his wallet to make sure it had been drawn on the State Street Trust.

He rose slowly, the small frown fixed above the bleak dark-green eyes. After a moment of hesitation, he put the statements and checkbook back where he'd found them and closed the drawer. He had already learned something he had not expected when he came, but he was a thorough man and now he continued on into the bedroom and gave it his inspection from the doorway: the mended spread on the double bed, the chest, a boudoir chair with its smudged arms, the combination vanity-dresser.

The medicine cabinet in the bathroom gave some idea as to just how little time Browning had spent there, for there were only two toothbrushes and paste, a razor, comb, pressurized can of lather, a bottle of ant-acid tablets. On a hook behind the door hung an old terry-cloth robe, beneath it a worn pair of pullman slippers.

The top drawer of the dresser yielded one clean white shirt, a red-and-green foulard tie, two handkerchiefs, a pair of shorts. The second and third drawers were empty but under some soiled shirts and shorts in the bottom one he found two thick Manila folders.

Very carefully then so as not to spill the contents, he removed first one and then the other and placed them on the bed, already conscious of his quickening interest. Turning back the cover of one folder he saw it contained perhaps a half inch of carbon copies; the second held a like quantity of photocopies. The headings, in capital letters, indicated that here were some quarterly reports or accountings of the Grayson Trust.

In themselves they told him nothing since he was not an accountant and had a hell of a time taking care of his own income-tax forms. The names and figures made up a list of stocks and bonds held by the estate together with the income produced and the current net value of each. As he skimmed the pages and their listings only one name stood out: Acme Investment Company.

He grunted absently as the three words clicked into the proper slot of his memory. That image brought a tight grin as he recalled that this fifteen-hundred-dollar monthly payment to the fictitious company went directly to Mona Vail. Because he knew it was a waste of time to try to decipher such records he tucked the folders under his arm, snapped off the light and went into the front room. He was nearly to the door when an idea came to him and he stopped and went back to the telephone stand.

Again he put the folders down so he could consult his little address book. When he had a number he dialed the home of a C.P.A. who had done a little work for him in the past.

"Harry," he said when he had an answer, "Jack Fenner . . . Yeah. Look, I got a rush job . . . I know you're busy; you're always busy. But this can't take long and you can charge time and a half, double time, for night work . . ."

He kept talking, cutting off the other's

protests by the force of his manner and his nonstop sales pitch.

"Just let me bring the stuff over, will you? If you can't handle it, okay . . . Yeah, but you can at least take a look, can't you? I'll be around to your place in less than a half hour so hang loose until I get there, hunh? See you then. 'Bye."

He was never sure what prompted his second telephone call from that apartment. It was probably a combination of things, the dominant one being the feeling that he had slipped up somewhere on a routine matter that he should have explored before. Again he consulted his little book and this time he sat down before he dialed the operator. When she came on he told her he wanted to place a credit-card, person-to-person call to Los Angeles.

His watch told him it was only eight o'clock—five in Los Angeles—and as he gave his number he said he wanted to speak to Mark Johnson.

He had never met the man and had become aware of him first when they both had worked for the national agency that had employed him. During that time there had been an occasional exchange of correspondence and two or three telephone conversations. Like himself, Johnson was now a private detective who preferred to operate alone, hiring help as needed. A couple of months back he had called Fenner and asked him to locate a witness supposed to be living in the city and Fenner had found her and passed along the necessary information.

Now, as the voice came to him from the other end of the line he said: "Mark? Jack Fenner. I was hoping I'd catch you before you left the office. How're tricks?"

"Hey, Jack. What do you know, boy? How is it on the East Coast? Keeping busy?"

Fenner replied and they talked a minute or so about this and that and then Fenner spoke his piece.

"I want you to find out what you can about a character named George Browning who worked out in your bailiwick maybe three or four years ago."

"Browning?" Johnson's tone sounded faintly sardonic. "That shouldn't be too tough. There can't be more than a hundred Brownings in the local book."

"So what? He wouldn't be in any book now anyway, would he? You'll have to go back to old books and I can give you a lead that should help."

"Let's have it."

"This guy once worked as a movie extra."

"Ahh! You mean he would have been listed with Central Casting."

"Also maybe he was a member of the Screen Actors' Guild. Central Casting would probably have an old address for him. I understand he did bits for Westerns. I think he worked for some used-car dealer when he didn't have a movie or TV job. See what you can come up with, Mark. Maybe you could make some phone calls this evening and follow up in the morning. I'll call your office at noon tomorrow your time, okay?"

"Fair enough. I should have something for you by then."

"Take it back as far as you can. From what I know of the guy he might even have a record. You might check that out, too, in case he has a rap sheet. If I need anything more I'll let you know tomorrow. Take care, kid. And thanks. I appreciate it."

He hung up and came to his feet, a new sense of encouragement working on him as he gathered his folders. The feeling lasted until he was out on the street and remembered what he had to do next.

16

When Jack Fenner had parked his car as close as he could to Alice Maxwell's apartment he was still reviewing his talk with his C.P.A. friend. His arguments had been forceful and he finally left the two folders with the promise that Harry would do what he could. Fenner had said that was all he asked. He didn't expect a thorough or precise report; all he wanted was an opinion. He made the further concession that even a guess from Harry would be better than nothing, adding that he would call Harry's office sometime in the morning.

Now, as he came down the third-floor hall, he was all too conscious that he had some unpleasant things to say to Carol Browning, at the same time warning himself to lead into the bad parts gradually after he had her confidence. He was ready for her when he knocked softly and then he nearly blew it all when Sam Carter opened the door.

For a long, incredulous moment he simply could not accept the reporter's presence. He had never been angrier in his life and in that first instant of outraged bewilderment he could feel that anger in the animal flutter in his back and knees. He was not sure whether the focus of his rage was Carter or the girl, and it took a tremendous mental effort to regain control of himself.

So he stood there, glaring and speechless, aware that Carter had his hat and coat on, hearing him mumbling that he was just about to leave. Somehow he kept his mouth shut until the door closed, reminding himself that any threat against Carter, or even an angry outburst, might well backfire. He gained time by looking at the closed door of the bedroom. He took off his coat and tossed it aside. When he turned and spoke his voice was tight and stony.

"Last night you told Kent and me that you'd keep your little hideout a secret."

"I didn't even mention you, either of you."

"How did Sam think you got here from Ufford? By carrier pigeon?"

"Oh, don't be so damn smart!" she said, her voice snapping. "I told him I was desperate for a place to go and I was a friend of Alice's from having been in your office several times. I said I came and asked if she could put me up, and she said yes. Sam couldn't possibly have known about you if you hadn't bumbled in just now like a dummy. You waited all day; why couldn't you have waited a few minutes longer?"

The accuracy of such reasoning took the steam out of Fenner and he felt a grudging respect for her rebuttal.

"Amen!" he said, completely off balance. "How right you are."

There was no reply to this and by now he could see that her color was still high, her smooth jaw set, defiant glints in the hazel eyes. This served to remind him that here was a woman who might rebel at any further such outburst and close him out entirely.

"Was Alice up when Sam came?"

"Yes, but she sensed we might want to talk privately and she was polite enough to say she was sleepy."

"So how did Sam know where to find you?"

"I called him."

"Why?" he asked, keeping his voice level and already knowing what the answer would be.

"I was alone in this damn room all day, that's why. I couldn't reach you. Every time I called Alice said you were out and you wouldn't call me and—"

She stopped as though aware that she would soon be shouting. "Why didn't you?" she demanded coldly. "What was so important you couldn't even make one call?"

"A lot of things. That's why I'm here now. You were lonely, hunh? Couldn't stand being cooped up even though you must have known what would happen if you were picked up."

"Well, you can just stop worrying about Sam Carter. I made him promise on the phone that he'd say nothing to anyone before I told him where I was. He's a friend. A good friend," she added defiantly. "I trust him."

"More than you trust Alan Hubbard?"

"Well, no."

"But not enough, is that it?"

"I couldn't call Alan for the same reason I wouldn't do it from Ufford. I was ashamed to show him just what a mess I'd made of things since we broke up. Can't you understand? I've got some pride left."

He studied her a moment as she sat there on the edge of the sofa-bed in her smart-looking navy dress. Her color was no longer noticeable and there was less determination in the angle of her jaw, the look in her eyes more challenging now than defiant.

He took his time lighting a cigarette when she refused his offer. He was still upset by what she had done and the risk she had taken so unnecessarily but he kept warning himself to take it easy. With this in mind he digressed without any preliminaries.

"Just why did you break up with Alan in the first place?"

"Because I was a stupid, spoiled brat and too young to appreciate him, that's why. I'd always had my own way and I guess I wanted a husband who would slap me down now and then when I had one of my little tantrums, someone to take charge, and say no sometimes and mean it.

"Alan was too much of a gentleman, I guess," she added, some remoteness showing in her gaze and the cadence of her voice. "We'd known each other quite a while and our families were friends, and I'd been secretly in love with him since I was fourteen or fifteen. I was the happiest girl alive for a while. He was sweet and attentive and there was nothing wrong when we were in bed either. But headstrong Carol wasn't ready to grow up. She had to have new excitements, trips, a continual round of parties. When I couldn't always have my way I'd nag him and taunt him and criticize, knowing I was being an unmitigated little bitch and wanting him to argue and shout back at me and maybe shake some sense into me.

"He wouldn't fight back," she said, "no matter what I did. He let me walk all over him. He just took it very patiently and politely like the perfect gentleman he is and that just seemed to aggravate me more. He never swore at me or slapped me. Maybe there was some small inferiority complex there where women were concerned that made him shy and reserved, but I was too stupid to understand that he could love me and still not fight with me once in a while. I wanted to be bossed sometimes, to be ordered about with a firm masculine authority. I never would have divorced him if he'd only tried to talk me out of it; I wanted to be talked out of it; I wanted to beg him to please say he'd fight to keep me, that he'd never give me a divorce in a million years. That's when my silly pride took over," she added regretfully.

"I took the first step and when he said all he ever wanted was my happiness, that if a divorce was what I wanted he wouldn't stand in my way, I couldn't back down. Don't you see?" she said, her voice softly miserable now. "I just couldn't make myself admit I was wrong and didn't really want a divorce, not then."

Her voice seemed to run down and Fenner, understanding how she felt and believing what he had heard was the truth, said: "I think he's still in love with you."

"I know," she said, head down now and the words muffled.

"How about you?"

"I guess so. I don't know." She looked up and tossed the blond hair out of her eyes, her face still with thought and the eyes withdrawn. "I think when I get out of this damn mess, if I ever do, I'll go away for maybe six months or so and do a little communing with myself. If I feel like I feel now I'll call him up and make a date. Maybe I'll be adult and sensible enough by then to come right out and ask him if he wouldn't like to try again."

Fenner nodded and put out his cigarette. "I guess you married George on the rebound."

"Spite would be a better word. I was absolutely furious with Alan. I didn't want to be on that damn dude ranch anyway. I hated it with all the creepy dames and the great outdoors. But I'd made my choice and I was stuck with it and George was there and very attractive, and he was so completely different from Alan —

"Oh, how do I know why I married him? He was big and good-looking, a dream on a horse. And he could play the guitar a little, and sing. I guessed he might be something

244

of a sexual athlete, and he was, and I must
have mistaken that sort of thing for love.
Maybe I was a little desperate and just didn't
care; maybe I wanted to bring him back
and flaunt him in Alan's face . . ."

She seemed to run down and Fenner
prompted her. "Did he ever tell you what he
did before he came to Nevada?"

"Just that he'd worked some in movies
and TV. Why?"

"I'm having a detective friend of mine in
Los Angeles check into his past a bit."

"What for, for heaven's sake? He's dead,
isn't he?"

"And we're trying to find out why, aren't
we?"

"Oh, I suppose so," she added
impatiently.

"What about Ufford? Did you phone
your uncle like I suggested?"

"Yes."

"You didn't tell him where you were?"

"Certainly not. You told me not to, didn't
you?"

"I told you not to call anybody but you
did . . . What did you tell him?"

"I said I wasn't going to tell anyone

where I was until he'd fixed it so I wouldn't have to go back."

"You told him the circumstances, how you got there?"

"Certainly. He told me about what happened to George and I made it sound like I couldn't believe it. I tried to sound shocked and scared, you know, pretending. He said he'd get in touch with Dr. Garic and see what he could do. He warned me I was just making matters worse by not coming to his office because the police suspected me and — oh, he gave me a good lecture. It was very tiresome."

"What did you tell him?"

"That I'd call him tomorrow."

Fenner nodded his approval and decided it was time he got to the hard part. He glanced at his nails and then at the closed bedroom door. He took a small breath, looking right at her now.

"What did Sam Carter have to say? Did he tell you about Frank Quinn?"

"Yes he did." She dropped her glance, her face obscured except for the slight puckering of her brows. "I'm terribly sorry, Jack. Really. I know he was a friend of yours, sharing an office and all. I always thought he was a nice little man, what I'd seen of him."

"You knew he was working for me last night too."

"I know."

"What did Carter tell you? How much?"

"Just that he'd been found in his car this morning. Somebody had shot him twice. Late last night, Sam thought. He said he'd talked with you and he somehow got the idea that you knew more about it than you were saying."

"Did he tell you what the police think?"

"Not exactly." She looked up then. Her eyes still seemed evasive but nothing showed in the still expressionless lines of her face.

"I'd already told Sergeant Gaynor of Homicide about Frank," Fenner said, "and what he was doing last night. He knew the situation, how I was supposed to be working for your husband. With what Gaynor had he was convinced that Frank saw someone he didn't tell me about, the killer, to be specific. He had to assume, and it was a sound assumption, that Frank saw a chance to collect on his information and made the mistake of taking it . . . What time did he get here last night?"

He spoke in the same even conversational tones and the words had an even greater impact because of this. There was a long, silent pause while the question was absorbed, the hazel eyes opening slowly as the shock and fear showed and the firm jaw went slack. He watched her wet her lips and swallow before she made a conscious effort to straighten her shoulders.

"Not long after you and Kent left," she said in shaky tones.

Fenner's voice was flat and cold with censure. "And you let him in, just like that!"

"Well, yes—" She tightened her lips and tried again. "What I mean is, this knock came and I thought I'd better ask who it was. He said he was from your office. I knew that. I thought you'd sent him."

"So you gave him a check for twenty thousand dollars."

This time her gasp was audible. The finger of one hand went to her lips as the color seeped from her cheeks.

"How—how did you know?" she whispered finally, her accents full of awe and consternation."

"The check was still on the body. Sergeant Gaynor has it. So just what do you think *he* thinks?"

"Oh—yes—" She took a breath and put the hand back in her lap. "I see. I guess your man Gaynor thinks I paid because if I hadn't Mr. Quinn would have told the police I'd been at my apartment when George was shot."

"That's close enough." Fenner leaned back, wondering how to go on from there. Before he could make up his mind she said:

"But it wasn't that way at all, Jack. It really wasn't."

"Okay. Tell me how it was."

"He said he'd seen this hippie come out of my apartment house. He said he didn't know who it was until you told him."

Fenner flinched inwardly and had time to curse himself again for his stupid mistake before she continued.

"He said he was willing to go to the police tomorrow—today—and tell them that he *had* recognized me, and that I had left my apartment *before* George ever got there. If he told them that and swore to it, it would clear me."

She took a small breath, fingers twisting in her lap now. "At first I didn't quite understand. When I did I asked him if he would just stand by and let me be tried for murder when he knew I didn't do it. He said no, he'd never go that far, but unless he cleared me I'd be arrested and questioned. With what the police had there would have to be a grand-jury investigation, and publicity, and all kinds of trouble for me. Any good lawyer would charge me a lot more than twenty thousand just to represent me that far, so why not pay now and avoid the whole sickening mess.

"Well"—her chin was out now and her old defiance was beginning to show in the cadence of her voice—"I thought, Why not? I could afford it. Pay the nasty little blackmailer and have done with it. Just what would you have done?"

For some obscure reason Fenner felt better and the grim tight lines in his angular face relaxed. What he had heard made a lot of sense and he was about to accept her explanation as true until, for some unaccountable reason, a new and disturbing objection seeped insidiously into his consciousness.

Wait a minute, Jack, he thought. *Did Frank Quinn actually recognize this woman as the hippie, or didn't he?*

He stood up abruptly and walked away from the bed-sofa. He wanted a drink, but Carol had already said there was no liquor in the house. He moved to the window and looked out into the unrevealing darkness as he began to think like a detective, not as he was today but as he was in the days when he had been a police officer, accepting nothing at face value, the suspicion always there about any suspect until the facts showed such suspicion to be groundless.

Frank Quinn had been evasive about just when the hippie had left the apartment. Purposely? If he had recognized Carol and assumed she could not have shot her husband, then what she had just told him might be true. But suppose, as had been assumed, that Quinn *had not* recognized Carol?

The news as to the hippie's true identity would have come as a complete surprise but it would still have opened up a possibility for a worthwhile demand for payment for his cooperation. He tried to put himself in Quinn's place, Quinn who was utterly convinced that his chance was coming if only he was patient; a big case that would give him the favorable publicity he sought, or some enormous fee that would perhaps give him freedom from the daily grind.

Frank could have said to himself: "Okay, Frankie, you didn't recognize the hippie and you can't pinpoint the time. You don't know if the girl killed her husband or not and you damn well don't care if she did. You can clear her by sticking to a story that says she left the building before her husband came. If she did kill him she'll sure as hell pay to get out of the box; if she didn't she'll pay just to avoid the grief that's sure to come. What difference does it make to you?"

Since Quinn's story to the girl did not in fact clear her, he realized such theorizing was pointless and now he tried another tack that had been working on his subconscious for some time.

Looking at the problem strictly from a

detective's viewpoint he understood that there were two or three ways he could figure how and why she had killed her husband. But with what he knew and had assumed there was no way he could picture her shooting Frank Quinn the night before. Admitting the possibility Joe Gaynor had suggested, that panic, hysteria, or whatever had prompted her to run without stopping to retrieve the check from Quinn's pocket; admitting all this, where, exactly, did she get the gun to do the job and where was it now?

He could ask Alice Maxwell tomorrow if there was a gun in the house but he could not believe this could be so. Alice with a hand gun in the house? Ridiculous . . .

"What?" he said, jerking his thoughts back to the moment and aware that Carol had spoken. "Sorry, I was thinking."

"That's what I was asking. What are you thinking?"

"For one thing, just what's the best way out of this for you."

"So what do you suggest?"

"It's time to turn yourself in."

"Tonight?"

"Tomorrow morning will do." He came back and sat down again, facing her now and seeing the skepticism in her gaze.

"I suppose I just go to Uncle Lamont's office and say, Here I am."

"Not quite. You phone him like you did today. You tell him exactly where to meet you and set the time—ten, ten-thirty—don't wait too long. You call a taxi to come to this address and you ride to some street corner—pick out a busy one—and Grayson will be there, believe me. He probably will already have arranged with the D.A. to bring you to his office. And you know the first question your uncle will ask you?"

"Where I've been since I walked away from Ufford."

"Right."

"And I tell him it's none of his business."

Fenner grinned in spite of himself, liking her spirit. "Right again. He'll ask you other things too before you get to the D.A. and you can tell him what you want. Grayson probably doesn't know about the check you gave Quinn, but the D.A. will and he'll want to know why you wrote it."

"What do I tell him?"

"Just what you told me and no more. He's going to keep throwing the when's and why's at you, but you don't have to answer and he knows that. Grayson probably wouldn't let you answer anyway."

"Will they arrest me?"

"I doubt it very much. At least not right away. I don't think the D.A. will risk it with what the police have, not someone with your standing, with an attorney like Grayson. They'll hammer away until Grayson calls a halt, maybe release you in his custody. At least temporarily. When they do, go back to your place and hang around until I get in touch."

He stood up, wanting to impress on her the importance of one point, yet not wanting to plead.

"Just remember this one point as a personal favor to old Jack, and your friend Kent Murdock; yes, and to your present roommate."

"I know," she said, brows arching as she rose and moved closer. "I'm never to tell where I've been or how I got here . . . But just remember I didn't tell Sam Carter that you brought me here."

Fenner's small grin was crooked and he was once again acutely conscious of how much he liked this girl.

"I'll have Murdock speak to Carter. And I like that word, never. Because you tell the truth and the rest of us are up to our neck in grief."

"Especially you?" she said, tipping her head slightly.

"Especially me."

"Would you like my promise in writing?"

"A handshake will do."

She gave him one, her hand soft and her grip firm. Before she released him she leaned close and kissed him lightly on the cheek before he could react. She said not to worry about her, please, and call her at home when he could.

17

Alice Maxwell was at her desk as usual when Jack Fenner arrived at his office at 9:30 the next morning. She had a lap full of heavy maroon yarn just beginning to take the shape of a sweater, and she gave him her cheerful good morning and her sweet smile. He asked if Carol Browning had been up when she left her apartment and she said yes.

"Up and dressed."

"Did any detectives come around here yesterday?"

"Oh, yes. Late in the afternoon. There's a note on your desk."

"Did they give you any trouble?"

"Not a bit. They were very nice. One was young and quite handsome. They just asked me a few questions about Mr. Quinn, like how he was to work for and what kind of a man was he, and did he have any trouble with anyone recently, or did I happen to overhear any threats—things like that.

"They wanted to know which was his office and they went in and spent maybe a half hour there, I suppose looking through his things. And oh, yes"—she took a slip of paper from her desk and offered it—"here are the addresses of Mr. Quinn's wife and brother."

He thanked her, walked halfway to his private office and stopped, his conscience bothering him and facing up to a subject he should have mentioned before.

"I guess you know Mrs. Browning is in a bit of trouble."

"Oh, yes. We talked quite a lot. She told me about being at Ufford, and of course I knew her husband had been murdered and that you thought it best for her to sort of hide out until you knew what should be done."

"Then I guess you know your boss may, the word is may, have put you on the spot with the authorities."

For a long second she just looked at him, her pretty eyes wide open before she replied.

"Oh, Mr. Fenner"—the innocence in her

voice and glance knocked him over — "I just don't believe that."

"Well, it's a fact just the same. Kent Murdock and I have deliberately stymied, temporarily at least, the official police investigation. And because of me you've had a sort of passive role in the scheme. If Mrs. Browning decides to tell them — she's turning herself in later this morning — where she's been the past couple of days — "

"Pooh! She won't say a word. Believe me, I know. She's a terrific person. Really, Mr. Fenner — why don't you marry her when things get straightened out? I know she likes you."

Fenner shook his head in slow amazement as he turned away. *Oh, brother,* he thought, *how wonderful to be young and have that kind of assurance and enthusiasm!*

At his doorway he stopped once more to put into words a question he had been reluctant even to think about.

"One question, Alice. It may sound silly to you, but don't let it bother you. All I need is a simple yes or no. Do you have a gun at your place? Did you ever have one?"

"A gun?" The word came out with a

bewildered gasp. "You mean like a pistol? Good gracious, no, Mr. Fenner. Why would I have a gun? I've never really seen one actually."

Afraid that she might say more he digressed swiftly. "Good," he said, trying not to show his relief. "Now will you get the Yellow-and-Black cab for me, please? I'd like to speak to a man named Marty; I don't know his last name."

One thing his years as a detective had done for Fenner was to enlarge the scope of his acquaintances in all walks of life. In the course of his career, official and private, he had poked his nose into many places. Probably only Kent Murdock, who had been on the streets with his camera for as many years, had a wider acquaintanceship, and this valuable accumulation of knowledge helped now as he talked to the day dispatcher of the cab company.

"Marty?" he said, "How're tricks?"

"No complaints, Jack. No complaints. So what's on your mind?"

"You got the trip sheets for last night's shift?"

"Right at my elbow."

260

"Okay, I'll bet you ten dollars you can't locate a driver who was out cruising around eight o'clock?"

"What else have I got to go on?"

Fenner named the street and address. "The driver I want was cruising west past that big apartment house at seven fifty-two when he picked up a fare."

"You got a bet."

"If you can get him to phone me at my office in the next few minutes you've got the ten and there's ten in it for him if he's got a halfway decent memory."

"You going to mail my ten?"

"The driver can pick it up at my office anytime today."

The bet was almost immediately productive. In less than five minutes Alice buzzed him and said some taxi driver was on the phone saying he was supposed to call. Fenner told her to put him on; then a hoarse voice was saying:

"This is Nick Rosseli. Marty said I was to call you. Are you the Fenner that used to work out of the 12th Precinct? Been private lately, haven't you? Sure," he said when Fenner confirmed his assessment, "I've had you for a fare plenty of times. Marty says you've got a sawbuck for me if I've got a good memory. Shoot. Try me."

Fenner repeated the details and the answer came quickly. "Sure I remember. The guy flagged me down in front of the apartment."

"What did he look like?"

"Good-sized, kinda old, looked like a banker, sort of red-faced, didn't say much."

"Where did you take him?"

"Corner of Adams and Blake. Northeast corner."

Fenner said Nick had the ten. "Stop by anytime and tell my secretary who you are. She'll have it ready."

He hung up, agate eyes full of thought and the beginnings of a smile working on his mouth. For the corner Nick had mentioned was but a step from the apartment building where Lamont Grayson lived. The banker type would fit nicely; it also would go with the French cuffs Fenner had seen on the hand holding the gun.

Not wanting to waste time speculating further, he asked Alice to get Harry, his C.P.A. friend.

"Hi, Harry," he said, coming directly to the point. "What can you tell me?"

"Nothing that I could swear to in court."

"We're not *in* court."

"What it looks like is two sets of records that add up to the same total assets. The heading says it's a trust fund and there's been a bit of shifting from one stock or bond to another."

"You mean one company was sold and another bought?"

"Right."

"What's wrong with that?"

"What's wrong is that there are too many companies that are unlisted. Not over-the-counter, not on the pink sheet. One or two you figure may represent privately held stocks, but this many transactions makes you wonder if some aren't phony. 'Course, like I said, that's only my guess. What do I do with this material?"

"Sit on it for now, Harry, and put your bill in the mail. I appreciate your nightwork. Maybe I can throw something bigger your way one of these days."

He sat back, the smile constant and very pleased with himself at the way things had worked out. Then, ticking off the items on his mental agenda, he buzzed Alice again and told her to get Hubbard & Company."

"They're on State Street, Alice. I'll hang on; just get me their operator."

He waited, hearing the dial clicks and presently a pleasant female voice said: "Good morning. Hubbard & Company."

"Is Mr. Alan Hubbard in?"

"One moment, please."

In hardly more than that a crisp and businesslike voice said: "Alan Hubbard."

"Jack Fenner, Mr. Hubbard. You asked me to get in touch if I found out anything about Mrs. Browning."

"Oh, yes. Yes." There was instant eagerness in the voice. "You've located her?"

"Sort of. But it's a bit too complicated to discuss over the phone. I was wondering if we could have lunch today."

There was a noticeable pause before a reply came and the words were tinged with a suggestion of apprehension and regret.

"Today? I'm sorry. I have a rather important client flying up from New York for a twelve-thirty lunch. If I'd known last night I might have postponed it but I'm afraid he's already on his way to the airport."

Fenner, swallowing his disappointment, quickly thought of another possibility.

"Is he coming to your office or are —"

"No. I'm meeting him at Lock Ober's. It's a favorite spot of his and he suggested it."

"Downstairs?"

"Yes, at the bar."

"Okay, how about meeting me there at noon. That should give us time enough before you meet him."

"Perfect. Perfect, Mr. Fenner. I'll see you at twelve."

Lock Ober's was an institution and had been for a great many years. It had a menu you could hardly hold in two hands and its prices were thought to be prohibitive by many people. But the chefs worked with great skill and the atmosphere, both downstairs and upstairs, was enough in itself to warn away those who had to look at the right side of the menu.

Fenner was standing at the bar, his drink

not yet ordered, when Alan Hubbard approached, and Fenner suggested a small table as far away from the congregation surrounding him as possible. When they were seated he asked what Hubbard would have and the reply was apologetic.

"I'm strictly a one-drink man at noon," Hubbard said, "and I'm afraid I ought to wait and join my two-straight-up-martinis client. But you go ahead, please . . . Now," he said, the eagerness in his blue eyes both obvious and engaging when Fenner had ordered, "what can you tell me about Carol? I've been worried sick about her. Is she all right?"

"She's meeting her uncle—probably has met him by now—and I imagine he took her down to talk to the District Attorney."

Hubbard started to speak, checked the thought, tried again. "Then if you know that you must have talked with her or know where she's been."

Fenner half closed an eye, his glance understanding. "That's a good guess."

"But you're not saying where?"

"It's a bit too complicated for that, Mr. Hubbard."

"The hell with this Mr. Hubbard stuff," Hubbard said, a somewhat unexpected comment for one who normally avoided profanity. "Alan, okay? What do you mean, complicated? You either know where Carol's been since she walked away from Ufford or you don't."

"I'll put it another way," Fenner said patiently. "There are too many people involved who just might be in a spot of trouble with the authorities if the truth comes out. Frankly, I don't think it ever will. I doubt if you'll get any more out of Mrs. Browning either." To get away from the subject he added: "Have you had a visit from the police yet?"

Hubbard made a small shrug of resignation, his glance straying. "Yes. Yesterday. It seems someone saw me go into Carol's place the night Browning was killed. They wanted to know why I was there, how long I stayed, things like that."

"You can blame me for the call. I had a man parked across the street to check on just who came and went. Actually he was there to see if Mrs. Browning showed. His name was Frank Quinn, Alan. A pretty nice guy, shared my offices. Do you know what happened to him?"

Hubbard thought a moment. "Wasn't a Frank Quinn—an attorney the paper said—found shot to death in his parked car?"

Fenner nodded and then, because he knew the questions would be coming, suggested the apparent reasons for Quinn's murder along with the police theory concerning it. He did not mention the twenty-thousand-dollar check that Carol Browning had given Quinn, but even without it Hubbard sensed the girl's possible involvement.

"Will the police question her about that too?"

"Probably. She's their number-one suspect. They have to figure that if she killed her husband, and Quinn saw her enter or leave the apartment at the right time, she could have killed him if he tried to blackmail her."

He stopped and made a point of looking at his watch. "We haven't much time," he said, "and there's not much more I can tell you anyway. So maybe *you'll* answer some questions."

"About what?"

"The Grayson trust."

"I'm afraid I don't know too much about it."

"Didn't Mrs. Browning ever show you any of the quarterly statements she got?"

"Some years ago, yes." The doubt still showed as he added: "Did you have anything specific in mind?"

"Is there any way Grayson could dig into that trust for his own use and still make the figures come out okay?"

"Do you think he did? You must have some reason for asking."

"While I was working for her, Mrs. Browning once told me she was worried about the estate. The income was holding up pretty well but the value kept shrinking."

"We were in that kind of a market for some time," Hubbard said. "Or weren't you aware of that?"

"All right," Fenner said good-naturedly, accepting the thrust. "I have a few shares of this and that I've accumulated. They aren't worth what they once were, but I like them

269

so I don't worry too much about it."

"You must also be aware that for a time interest rates climbed to ridiculous heights; unheard-of might be a better word."

"Agreed."

"In the Grayson case I can give you one sound reason for the shrinkage aside from a falling market. Carol's father had perhaps a third or more of his holdings in tax-exempt bonds, which were at the time he bought them a sound investment. These income bonds were sold to pay three and a half, three and five-eights percent at par, about all any high-grade bond paid at the time.

"Well," he said as though the answer was too obvious to mention, "Mr. Grayson bought many such bonds at par. Unless they were sold some years ago the estate had to suffer. Because the same-quality bond could be bought recently with a five, five-and-half coupon, if not more."

He sat back, the discourse concluded. "Those bonds, which cost a thousand, could be bought a year ago at anywhere from the high sixties to the middle seventies. In other words, if there was a half million in such bonds in the estate originally they might bring no more than three hundred and fifty thousand at current prices."

"All right," Fenner said. "We've got eight minutes left, so answer my first question. Could Grayson dip into that fund and get away with it?"

"Certainly." The reply came at once and then Hubbard qualified it. "But not indefinitely."

"How?"

"Several ways. Suppose I give you one example . . . under the terms of the trust, Lamont Grayson had authority to manage, to buy and sell at his discretion. He could not be held responsible for his judgment unless it could be proved frivolous or with some intent to defraud. What he could do if he intended to steal, for whatever reason, would be simply to sell legitimate securities and buy hot ones to replace them."

"Ahh—" Fenner said, a new light dawning.

"Exactly. Security thefts have mushroomed. Some of the mostly highly respected banks and brokerage houses, mostly the brokerage houses, have reported fabulous losses of securities they were holding or exchanging. Some have gone unreported in fear of bad publicity. No one can guess at the total because not all such thefts make the newspaper columns."

"Okay. Give me an example, a hypothetical case. Say Grayson takes two or three hundred thousand and wants to make sure it won't show."

"He simply sells sufficient bonds or whatever, and buys back the same amount of a similar stolen security for twenty-five percent on the dollar and pockets the difference."

"How, without being caught? Do they pass these certificates or bonds around like trading stamps? Isn't there any record?"

"Most bonds were coupon bonds. Anyone could clip a coupon and collect the interest. But if a major theft is reported, a notice will go around to all banks and brokers saying that so many bonds of such and such issue are missing and to report any large transfers — you see, in order to collect you have to find a buyer for the bond. And in many cases one bond could well be issued with a face value of fifty thousand or more. A man with a vault full of one-thousand-dollar bonds could probably sell them one at a time forever."

"Then if Grayson sold any large denomination bonds he'd probably get nailed."

"Eventually. But he wouldn't have to sell to profit. He'd simply list the hot bonds as assets, pay the interest regularly, out of his own pocket when it came due, or credit that interest to the estate. The bonds, hot or not, show as assets until someone tries to sell them. Meanwhile they make damn good collateral. A man of Grayson's standing could simply hand them to his bank, sign a note at the going interest rate, and they'd credit his account with maybe eighty percent of the current value."

Fenner nodded thoughtfully as his mind took the next step. "What happens on the fifteenth when Grayson hands over the estate?"

Hubbard grunted softly, the blue eyes amused. "I should imagine his accounts will be subjected to a pretty thorough audit. Some good C.P.A. firm, and probably a broker, will inventory things and you can be sure they'll double-check everything on the·

list. To make sure, and for the later use of the Internal Revenue people, they'll want broker's slips showing the purchase price of everything there.

"Because every transaction is going to show either a profit or a loss. If it's a profit you have to declare it on your income-tax return; if it's a loss you want to take advantage of it. So you keep your 'buy' and 'sell' orders because the Internal Revenue boys are not going to take your word for it. That's where the hot bonds, if any, will show up since there won't be any legitimate 'buy' orders with the date of purchase, price, commission charges, to establish a tax basis . . ."

He glanced up as he finished, the focus of his attention some distance away. He pushed back his chair.

"Sorry to have to run like this, but I see my man has arrived." He put his hand on Fenner's arm. "And thanks for telling me about Carol. She'll be all right, won't she?"

"If her uncle is worth a damn as counsel," Fenner said, wishing he felt as confident as he sounded. "And thanks for the brief seminar on bond manipulation."

Hubbard's grin was quick and genuine as he shook hands, and Fenner felt a pleasant inner glow at the firmness of the grip and what seemed like approval in the directness of Hubbard's glance. Now, as he walked away he reminded himself to put in a good word for his new-found friend when he talked to Carol. He might even suggest that it would be a good idea to remarry him.

18

Lamont Grayson lived in one of the older and more sedate cooperative apartment buildings west of the city center and not far from the river. Fenner had known there would be a doorman who had to be by-passed and he chose the direct approach.

He had dressed that morning with an appointment with Alan Hubbard in mind, and because of this he had selected a medium-gray business suit, well tailored and conservative so that he would be just as well dressed for the meeting as he knew Hubbard would be. He even added a gray snap-brim hat, a concession he seldom made these days unless it was raining. Now, swinging in under the marquee, the picture of confidence and efficiency, he nodded to the uniformed guardian without slowing down.

"From Mr. Grayson's office," he said. "I have his key."

"Yes, sir." The doorman offered a small salute without hesitation. "Five-A."

Fenner said he knew and went on to the elevators, pleased with his performance and nurturing some small feeling that something good would come from the trip. The fifth-floor corridor was empty and it took but a few seconds to pick the lock.

Since he had called Grayson's office and learned his man was in before hanging up, he entered with confidence and took a quick look about the living room. He had never been here before but research had told him it was a six-room apartment which Grayson had bought some years ago for himself and his wife, and Grayson had continued to live there even though there was much too much room for a man who seldom entertained at home.

The living room was spacious and tastefully furnished but it had somehow an empty unlived-in look and after his first quick inspection he saw that there was only one piece here that might hold something interesting. This was a heavy mahogany secretary and he opened the desk part and went through the pigionholes before examining the drawers.

He had no sound reason for his search but in the back of his mind was a nagging but nebulous idea based on the hunch that Grayson had been using the estate to his personal advantage. His accountant friend had suggested the possibility of a double set of books and why should this be if all was in order. The approach of the fifteenth, the settlement date, gave some substance to his hunch and when he found nothing of interest in the secretary, he went on to the first bedroom.

This, feminine in character, looked as if it hadn't been used since the wife had departed. The second one was sufficiently disordered to suggest recent occupancy and the first thing he noticed were the two lightweight suits on the bed — one dark gray and one medium — very neat on their hangers; a pile of shirts, some neckties. When the highboy drawers revealed nothing but articles of clothing, he went to the closet. There were four matching pigskin bags well back against the wall, expensive-looking and darkened with usage. The smallest felt empty and he left it. The medium-sized one made him grunt and felt as if it was filled with books.

He dragged it out, hope building swiftly inside him. He put it flat on the floor, snapped off the two catches and discovered the center one was locked. This too was encouraging, and while it would have been simple to force the lock, he took time to select a tiny, hooked arm on his lock-picking gadget and do the job properly.

What he saw when he opened the lid was money. Stacks of it. Some bundles had fifty-dollar bills on top, some had hundreds, but he touched nothing since he was not interested in amounts—his first guess said maybe two or three hundred thousand—but only in the fact that the currency was here ready for flight.

He remained there on one knee for a minute or so, bright glints in his eyes as some new sense of accomplishment made itself felt. He took an unconscious breath and held it momentarily before exhaling softly. Then he relocked the case, snapped up the catches, replaced it, and returned to the living room.

Unable to put down the fast-forming hypothesis in his brain, and recalling now the airline folders he had seen on Mona Vail's desk, he sat down by the telephone and got out his little address book. He had two names here of airline employees of some importance and he was speculating on his problem by putting himself in the position of a man who was going to run, possibly, it occurred to him, with a blond dish called Mona Vail. Having decided on two or three likely destinations, he dialed the airline whose insignia he had recognized when he had made the drink for Mona Vail.

"Mr. Watkins, please," he said when the office operator answered. He got another female voice who wanted to know who was calling and he told her. Another few seconds and he had his man.

"Hi, Jack," the cheerful voice said. "Where do you want to go this morning?"

Fenner said what he wanted was information and Watkins laughed and said he thought so.

"You can do me a big favor if you'll check over your reservations for the next couple or three days."

"To where?"

Fenner had been doing a lot of very fast thinking about that very same thing and he'd made a couple of conclusions. Grayson had lived many years in Europe. It was familiar ground. He might also be aware because of his background, that when his embezzlement was uncovered Europe would be the first place the law would look for him. With the help of Interpol he might not be too hard to find, since of all the countries Switzerland would be the one to accept that much currency without asking too many embarrassing questions.

Brazil was better and safer. That's where embezzlers had gone in the past since there was no extradition. The only other possibility seemed to be Panama, which was almost as free-wheeling in the currency market as Switzerland.

"South," he said finally.

"Florida?"

"Farther. Panama or Brazil."

"No direct flights from here."

"So we change at Kennedy. A guy would still be better off buying space straight through, wouldn't he?"

"You got a name?"

"Grayson or Vail. Maybe one seat, maybe two."

Watkins said to let him check and Fenner kept asking himself questions and trying to answer them. He had accepted the figure of three hundred thousand just to have something to work with. Why would a man with that much cash keep it in his bedroom closet? Why not a safe deposit box?

Because you could only get it out between ten and three and not at all from Friday afternoon to Monday morning. Tuesday was the fifteenth. Payday. And today was—by God—today was Friday!

"Yes," he said eagerly as Watkins said: "Jack? . . . We've got a Vail. Two seats."

"To where?"

"Panama."

"When?"

"Tonight. Ten o'clock with an hour to change at Kennedy."

"I love you."

"I know you do."

"Dinner for you and your wife any night you name."

Watkins said he would make a note of

that and consult the boss and Fenner thanked him again and left the apartment whistling softly. He felt so good he saluted the doorman and that gentleman returned the salute and asked him if he got what he wanted.

"I sure did," Fenner said happily. "I sure did."

By the time Jack Fenner was back downtown he felt like three martinis and an expensive lunch, but because he still had things to do he settled for a lot less: a hamburger and a beer at a bar and grill not far from the *Courier* building.

There was a telephone booth here with a door so one could close himself in, and Fenner made himself wait until he had finished his beer before he went inside and got out his credit card. He had told Mark Johnson in Los Angeles he would call at noon and it was still a little early by Pacific Time but worth a try. Once again his luck was in and when Johnson answered he asked how he'd done.

"Not too bad," Johnson said, "thanks to

that lead you gave me."

"The Central Casting thing."

"Right. It opened up a few things."

"Okay, give."

"Your man Browning was a real high-type character around these parts, the wife-beater sort. She had him pulled in twice and then refused to appear against him. The last time he broke her jaw and cracked three ribs so when she had him arrested she pressed charges. He got sixty days."

"Did he serve it?"

"Appealed. But I guess he figured he had run out the string in these parts—you were right about his being a used car salesman—because he grabbed six hundred bucks of his employer's dough and took off. The larceny warrant is still outstanding if it matters. What's he done in your town?"

"He got himself killed."

"It figures."

"What about the wife that took the beatings?"

"Oh, she's living in Venice. A waitress. Living with a bartender down there."

"Divorced?"

"Not that she knows of."

"Don't tell me you talked to her."

"Why not? You wanted a rundown on the guy. It's all part of the picture, isn't it? We aim to please out here . . . I asked her about a divorce and she said no. She didn't want to know where he was or what he was doing, and maybe she'd divorce him someday and maybe not. Said she never had any notice from him or an attorney so she guessed she was still married and to hell with him."

"Thanks, Mark. You did a job."

"It was what you wanted?"

"That and more. How much do I owe you? And don't be modest."

"How about fifty."

"Is it enough?"

"It wasn't too tough. I did a lot of it, except for the Venice trip, right here sitting on my duff with a phone in my hand. Fifty will be fine."

Fenner said it would be in the mail in the morning, adding that he hoped he could do something for Johnson someday at his end of the country. Johnson said he'd keep it in mind.

19

One advantage Jack Fenner found in Kent Murdock's move from the streets to his job of picture chief was that he could generally be found during working hours. Now, thinking hard about Mark Johnson's information and well satisfied with what he had learned, he moved into the *Courier's* small lobby off the local classified department and stepped into the elevator.

An ancient pensioner took him to the third floor and he went along a corridor, past the art department, and into a longish room, now deserted, with calcimined walls that were scarred and penciled. There were a few small battered desks, a pipe-rack frame for coats, a steel cabinet for cameras, lenses and equipment, and at the immediate right a cubby that had been partitioned off in one corner of the main room.

This was Murdock's daily domain, its

furniture a desk, an extra chair, one window; a two-way radio was perched on a corner of the desk, a duplicate of the one in the city room. A monitor sat on top of the radio and the three tiny lights glowing here indicated that three of the six company radio-station wagons were in use.

Murdock was on the phone as Fenner propped himself against the door frame and unbuttoned his coat. When Murdock hung up he marked something on the daily assignment sheet before he glanced up, his eyes darkly curious but nothing showing in his face.

"Busy?"

"Not very."

"Do you know an office with a telephone where we can talk? Not this sweatbox."

The insult brought a grin and Murdock said: "Sure," and stood up to back Fenner out of the doorway. "You look," he added, "like a guy who's just discovered a sure way to beat the horses. Come on, I can't wait to get the formula."

He led the way, using the stairs for the one-flight climb to the editorial offices. A low railing guarded the wide expanse of city room and he turned left before he came to it, moving along a row of small offices until he came to a frosted glass panel that said: *Drama* and underneath this: *Television-Radio.*

There were two desks here angling across the corners, one cluttered and the other practically bare; two swivel desk chairs, two spares, a dented filing cabinet, and an old open bookcase with shelves of magazines and assorted papers.

"These guys won't be in until later," Murdock said, his gesture encompassing the room, "choose your seat. Now what's so hush-hush."

"It's not hush-hush, I just don't want to be interrupted. Let's talk about Sam Carter."

"Carter?" Murdock's surprise showed. "Why?"

"I'll come to that."

"All right, let's."

"Carter came from the West Coast. L.A. right?"

"Right."

"Call personnel and find out just when."

Murdock thought a moment, a frown

beginning to show. "I don't have to. It was two years February."

"You know the paper he worked for out there?"

"The L.A. *Gazette.*"

"Would you happen to know anyone working for that paper?"

Again the moment of thought. "As a matter of fact I do. A youngster named Walker. He went to school in the east, came here as an office boy, graduated to general assignment. His old man was an engineer who got transferred to the Coast and when the family moved Walker went along. I still get a card from him maybe once a year."

Fenner put his telephone credit card on the desk. "Call and see if he's in. Use this."

Murdock made no move to touch the card. He leaned back, the swivel springs squeaking with his weight. He eyed Fenner steadily for five seconds.

"Just what do I ask Walker?" he said with some suspicion.

"What he knew about Carter. Habits, what kind of a job he did, why he quit—or was fired."

Murdock did not like the request; he said

so. "I don't like it. Why should I pry into Sam's private life or his past?" He sat up abruptly, his dark eyes narrowing with disbelief as some new thought prompted him. "You're not suggesting Sam had anything to do with this murder business?"

"I'm not suggesting. I just want to get all the facts I can."

"No."

"You'd rather just sit there and let Carol Browning sweat the thing out?" It was Fenner's turn to lean forward, to argue with spirit and determination. "It was Carter's gun."

"He's already admitted that; he told us why it was there."

"He had reason to resent Browning and I think I might have another reason that could tie him in; that's why I want to know all I can about him before I go any farther."

Murdock's grunt had a scornful inflection. "Come off it, Jack. Whatever Carter was on the Coast, he's been a damn good newspaperman here—read his weekly crime expose—but there's no violence in the man."

"Others who've shown no violence for

forty years have hacked their wives and kids to death with an ax. You know that as well as I do. Who can say who's going to be violent under certain circumstances?"

"But dammit! You must have something more than some wild suspicion."

Fenner saw the disapproval in his friend's expression and knew he had better lay it all on the line.

"Carter's from Los Angeles, right?"

"So?"

Browning's from the same area."

"He is? I thought Nevada."

"Before Nevada. I had a colleague of mine out there check him out," he said and repeated what Mark Johnson had told him.

By the time he had finished Murdock was sitting erect, the look of narrowed suspicion no longer showing.

"Jesus!" he said softly. "So that's the kind of bastard poor Carol married."

Fenner kept punching. "Do you believe in coincidence?"

"You know damn well I do. I've seen it happen too often."

"Two guys from the same town. One was a wife-beater and thief. The other a newspaperman who got around, who could easily have read or heard about Browning's arrest, maybe the larceny warrant. There could have been a lot more we don't know about."

Murdock shrugged, not yet convinced. "It's possible but —"

Fenner cut him off. "Remember I told you I was going to case Browning's hideout? Well here's one thing I found that you don't know about."

He went on quickly then, explaining about the monthly five-hundred-dollar-check Browning had been cashing for someone.

"What other reason could there be but blackmail? Who did the payments go to but someone who knew his past and could blow the whistle to his wife that maybe he wasn't even legally married to her?"

Such arguments were convincing. That Murdock was impressed was now obvious but he still had reservations.

"With only Browning's endorsement on those checks who's to say who they went to? You can't prove they went to Carter — coincidence or no coincidence."

"Not until the police subpoena his bank records and deposits."

"He wouldn't have to deposit that five hundred each month, even if he had collected."

"They could use the same method the Internal Revenue guys do. If Carter makes ten here and his income or standard of living shows he's been getting fifteen, he has to explain how. Carter lives pretty good. He drives an eight-thousand-dollar Mercedes—"

"He bought it for fifty-five secondhand," Murdock said, still hanging tight.

"I've heard he gambles."

"Some."

"I've seen him at the track in the season."

"So have I."

"What about those poker games?"

"Once a week. Mostly with guys from the shop. Twenty-five and fifty. Cents. You can lose, if you're a lousy player, maybe seventy-five, eighty bucks a night."

"Call L.A.!" Fenner said flatly, his patience wearing thin. "If you don't by God I will. Walker, you say this friend's name is. What the hell is the matter with you? Are you afraid of what you might turn up? . . . Give me the phone!"

He reached for it and Murdock's reaction was quick. He grabbed Fenner's wrist and his grin was sheepish as he took the telephone away from him.

"Okay," he said, taking no offense at Fenner's outburst. "Maybe it's better to give the idea a try than to keep yelling at each other."

He dialed, got an outside line, read off Fenner's credit-card number, and said he wanted to make the call person to person. He got comfortable as the operators went to work, pulling out a drawer and hooking an instep on the edge, his lean face relaxed and at ease.

"Hello," he said presently. "Eddie? Kent Murdock here on the *Courier*. Yeah. Your old trainining ground. That's right. How the hell are you?"

He turned his back on Fenner and directed his gaze out the lone window as he came to the point.

"I want to ask you about a guy that used to work on your sheet. I think you must have known him back a couple years ago.

Sam Carter . . . Yeah, that's right. Yes . . . Yes, he's been with us ever since; doing a good job, too. Look, can you tell me why he left the *Gazette?* Did he quit or was he —"

He cut the sentence off and Fenner, seeing only the profile could see worry lines start to form around the eyes as Murdock nodded absently from time to time. This went on for fully two minutes before Murdock grunted and said:

"I didn't know it was that bad." Another pause. "I can see why . . . Yeah, I understand. Strictly confidential, Eddie, and thanks."

He removed his foot and kicked the drawer shut. He let the chair-spring bring him upright and wound up the conversation.

"Well, if you ever should happen to get this way be sure and drop in. I'm always good for some drinks and a free meal . . . Righto."

He cradled the instrument with slow deliberation, swung his chair to face Fenner. He reached for a cigarette, a tight, hard smile at the corners of his mouth. When he had a light he said:

"You were right about the gambling. He

must have reformed because he got in way over his head out in L.A.''

"Bookie trouble?"

"Right. And the funny thing is it wasn't the horses or dice; it was football games, pro and college. He was a nut who thought he could beat the odds. The word got around that he was in a little trouble from time to time, but what blew the whistle was those annual New Year's Day college bowl games. He had 'em all — the wrong way.

"How," he asked, his expression wry and mildly incredulous," would you like to start out New Year's Day morning reasonably solvent and wind up thirty-eight hundred bucks in the hole at the end of the day?"

For a long moment Fenner could only stare with brows bunched as he considered the figure and began to realize the implications of such a loss to a professional bookmaker.

"Thirty-eight hundred?" he said with growing wonderment. "And he couldn't pay off?"

"No way, according to Eddie. He called the office that night and told them his father was seriously ill in New York and that he'd have to leave for a few days. He never came back."

"Just took off, hunh?"

He fell silent then, his mind groping, glad of this new information but somewhat discouraged when he realized that in itself it need not be important. He watched Murdock rise and move over to stare out the window. Finally, forcing his thoughts on, he got out his address book and reached for the telephone.

It was with some feeling of guilt that he dialed Carol Browning's number and he found it hard to rationalize his neglect these past few hours. The sound of her voice was like a tonic and quick relief flooded through him now that he understood that she had not been formally arrested and charged.

"Hey, it's good to hear your voice," he said. "I told you they wouldn't hold you. Was it rough?"

"Just where have *you* been?" she replied, sounding more severe than angry. "I called your office twice—don't you ever let your secretary know where you can be reached? What kind of a detective are you anyway? As a matter of fact I expected to find you lurking outside the District Attorney's office ready to comfort me and hold my hand."

"Your uncle must have done a good job."

"He was wonderful. The District Attorney got very angry with him, but Uncle Lamont just sat there and smiled at him."

"Did Grayson ask where you'd been all that time?"

"Naturally. I told him it was none of his business."

"The D.A. too?"

"Oh, he only asked me about nineteen times," she said lightly. "It really wasn't too bad . . . what have you been doing to help me?"

"Lots of things. That's why I'd like to come over." He glanced at his watch. "How about five o'clock? I'd like to see your uncle too and—"

"Well, you don't have to worry about that. He's coming by then for a drink."

"Okay to bring Kent Murdock?"

"I'd hate you if you didn't."

"I'll bring him, Carol . . . see you."

He cradled the instrument and when he

looked up Murdock was regarding him with half-closed eyes. "What was that all about?"

"I've had a busy day," Fenner said with a touch of smugness. "In the process of my travels and investigations I learned some things about Mr. Lamont Grayson you won't believe; I think they'll surprise Carol Browning even more. But since I'm not going to speak my piece twice, you're invited to come and listen in. How about calling Sam Carter?"

"Why?" Murdock asked, his reluctance showing.

"I want to talk to him."

Murdock started to speak, reconsidered, tried a new approach. "I've been thinking," he said and the humps and wrinkles in his brow seemed to bear this out. "Why, assuming Sam was hitting George Browning for five hundred a month regularly, would he kill the goose that was laying the golden eggs? Suppose even that he knew Browning was going to get a fat divorce settlement and intended to hit him for one big and final touch in return for his silence. Why the hell would he kill him first?"

"I don't know," Fenner said truthfully. "That's what stops me cold. So why not talk to him? If you're sensitive you can leave the room, old buddy."

For a second or two he thought his friend was going to turn stubborn on him, but he finally reached for the telephone and asked the operator for Carter's desk. After a bit he covered the mouthpiece with his hand.

"He's not in."

"How do you leave word?"

"What word?"

"For him to meet us at Carol's apartment at five, or as soon he can make it. If he has the customary news hawk's oversized bump of curiosity he'll come running."

Murdock relayed the message to the operator and then asked for the city desk. "Al," he said a moment later. "Kent Murdock. Will you get a message to Carter when he comes in, in case the operator misses him? Yeah. Tell him to get over to Mrs. George Browning's place by five if he can. He knows the address. Right." To Fenner he said: "Okay, mighty man of mystery. Let me get back to my desk for a few minutes and get someone to take over."

20

When Carol Browning opened the door of her apartment her hazel eyes went wide and she gave Fenner the biggest smile he had ever seen.

"Come in, come in," she said, swinging the door wide. "Am I glad to see you . . . and Kent too. Come in."

They stepped inside, both of them grinning at the welcome. Murdock, who knew his way around, opened the entryway closet and he and Fenner got rid of their hats and coats. As they came down into the living room she pointed to a cupboard-like antique on the other side of the room.

"I think you'll find everything you need there and let's get at it. Scotch for me, please. A touch of water."

They went over and made their drinks, Murdock sitting beside her on the divan and Fenner taking a cushioned chair facing them. He was still smiling inside at the enthusiasm of her welcome and it took a minute to sober up for the task ahead. He waited until he had taken a swallow and she spoke first.

"You know, I really didn't believe you last night."

"Believe what?"

"That if I turned myself in they wouldn't arrest me. Oh, that District Attorney wanted to all right. You could tell that, but with Lamont there challenging each and every one of his threats I think he was afraid to. Not that I expect that will be the end of it. But right now it's enough that I can sleep in my own bed tonight for a change . . . Have you found anything else?"

"A few things. I talked to your stepbrother."

"Oh, Barry? Does he know where I've been?"

"I filled him in. He'll probably be around before too long. I also talked to your ex."

"Oh?" The reference to Alan Hubbard made her thoughtful. "What did he have to say?"

"He gave me a dissertation on the effect

of high interest rates on income bonds that were bought at par."

"Yes," she said. "I imagine he did. I've heard it . . . And what have you been doing, Kent?"

"Arguing with Jack."

"Arguing? About what?"

"I think he's got a couple of theories about the murder of your husband. He hasn't come right out and said so, but I think that's one reason he wanted to see your uncle."

The buzzer cut him off and when the girl went to open the door, Lamont Grayson walked in, his smile fading as his glance took in the others.

"Company?" he said a little stiffly. "You did say five, didn't you?"

"Of course I did. They phoned after I talked with you. Take off your coat and get comfortable."

Grayson didn't bother with the closet. He slipped out of his oxford gray topcoat, put it on an occasional chair near the entrance, placed his homburg on top of it.

"Fix yourself a drink," Carol said. "I think a little celebration is in order."

"Not just now, Carol," Grayson said, finding a seat. "And I'm not so sure this celebration, as you call it, isn't a bit premature. If you'd only stop being stubborn and tell where you were and how you got there, I'd perhaps have more to work with."

The girl sipped her drink and shrugged. "Sorry, Lamont. I'm afraid that will have to remain a deep, dark secret," she said and gave Fenner a quick, sly wink.

Grayson continued to appear ill at ease and Fenner noticed a sort of wariness in his look as he glanced at Murdock and then back. Deciding he might as well get on with it, Fenner said:

"I'm glad you stopped by. I've been wanting to talk to you."

"Really," Grayson said, still stiff. "Why?"

"To tell the truth I've been working up a motive that might tie you in on that murder the other night."

He watched the narrowness grow in the other's eyes, saw him give the woman a long hard look."

"That's very interesting," he said dryly. "And did you find one?"

" I think so . . . You didn't get what you wanted last night in George Browning's little love nest, did you?"

"What love nest? I'm afraid I don't know what you're talking about."

Fenner took his time. He put his glass aside and lit a cigarette, turning the lighter over in his fingers as he inhaled. He was quite sure that Grayson was his man. The description given him by the taxi driver, the destination of that particular ride, the fact that Grayson's neat French cuffs were again visible, these things seemed enough to make accusation valid.

"What I'm wondering is where you got the gun you held on me. Did you pick it up at home or did you have it in your office?"

By now he was aware of the blank look in Carol's eyes and even Murdock had a puzzled frown. Before he could continue the buzzer again demanded attention. This time he answered it because he was closer.

"Hi," Sam Carter said, advancing slowly, his bespectacled eyes busy as they took in the room before fixing on Murdock.

"I got your message. Hope I'm not late for the party."

He didn't take his coat off and he was wearing no hat. Murdock asked him if he knew Grayson. Carter nodded and said he knew who he was although he didn't think they'd met. Grayson said nothing as Carter found a chair, his glance quizzical and a bit uncomfortable as he waited for someone to clue him. Fenner obliged.

"I was talking to Mr. Grayson about the Browning murder and a funny experience I had last night. I had a hunch — I'll tell you how I got it in a minute — that Browning knew Grayson had been dipping into the trust fund he was handling for Carol."

Grayson leaned forward slowly, more color showing in his florid face, his angry gaze fixed, his graying mustache fluttering.

"Now just one damn moment, Fenner. You talk like that in front of witnesses and you're in trouble."

"That's a chance I have to take. Why don't you hear me out and then see if you think you can take any action."

He paused to address the room; then went

on to tell what had happened when he entered Browning's apartment and came up against someone with a flashlight and a gun. He gave the dialogue as he remembered it, spoke of the view from the front window as the man flagged a Black-and-Yellow cab.

"I called the dispatcher in the morning and luckily the driver had the notation on his trip sheet. The description fit Mr. Grayson, and now I'll tell you what I think you were after . . . Let's start with your confidential secretary, who was sleeping with Browning from time to time . . . This I know," he added when Grayson started to interrupt, "because I checked all that out when I was working for Carol—times, dates, the whole bit.

"So I got this wild idea," he said. "That secretary wouldn't exactly be a candidate for a beauty queen—I've seen her, you know—and I wondered why a guy like Browning, who certainly could do a lot better, would be fooling around with her like that. I finally came up with a possibility. With Browning dead and the estate settlement but a few days away, I decided to have a look at that apartment, and sometimes hunches pay off. "This one did."

"Now see here," Grayson said, sputtering now. "If you think — "

"I'm almost through," Fenner cut in. "If I hadn't walked in on you, I'd never have known if the hunch was any good or not. But that time I got lucky. You hadn't searched as far as the bedroom and that's where I found them."

"Found what, Jack?" Carol said before Grayson could speak.

"A carbon of one of the quarterly statements that Grayson sent you. There was also another folder with photocopies of a similar statement that didn't seem to tally with the first."

He went on to explain how he had delivered both folders to his accountant friend and repeated the information that had been given him.

"So don't tell me there were no such statements. I have them. I found them just where I said I did — how else would I get them?"

He paused again, seeing the color start to seep from Grayson's florid cheeks. The look of challenge and resentment that had been present became apprehensive and uncertain as he leaned back in his chair. He seemed to be having trouble deciding what to say next. Finally, he cleared his throat.

"Assuming there were such statements. What exactly do they prove?"

"There was one item that I happened to notice," Fenner said, ignoring the question. "A monthly payment of fifteen hundred bucks to the Acme Investment Service."

"What about it? Payment for investment advice is a legitimate expense, chargeable to the trust."

Fenner's grunt was a sardonic sound in the otherwise quiet room.

"Come on, Grayson," he said, deciding it was time to drop the Mister. "What investment advice did you hope to get from Mona Vail? I found out about those payments to your blond friend way back when I was working for Carol. She admitted it when I talked to her the other morning. Eighteen thousand a year to her, twelve thousand more to your wife—"

"Could I ask a question?" Carol Browning was leaning forward, her empty glass in both hands. "I guess we knew about Mona Vail, but how could Uncle Lamont know George had those statements."

"Easy," Fenner said, still watching Grayson. "George told him."

"Why?"

"Because George, with that secretary's help, had found out that your uncle had been juggling that trust of yours for his benefit. My guess is that on settlement day he'll be a few hundred thousand short. Browning wanted a cut. He must have told Grayson that before he was killed." He looked back at Grayson and put the next question with brutal directness. "How much cash have you got in that suitcase?"

He could see the fear and consternation in the other's eyes now. The air of aloofness and confidence that was Grayson's personal trademark had vanished, leaving him aged and defenseless.

"What suitcase?" he said, stammering in his attempt to sound angry.

"That middle-sized pigskin job you've got packed in your bedroom closet."

Fenner saw then that Grayson wasn't the only one who was surprised. Murdock was peering at him as though he were a block away and Carol was watching with open-eyed amazement; Sam Carter looked puzzled and confused. He also realized one other thing: in spite of their reactions they sensed that he was not kidding.

"I didn't count it," he said. "Fifties and hundreds. Stacks of 'em."

"Why?" the question came from the girl rather than Grayson. "I mean, why would he want all that cash?"

"Because if he stayed he knew he'd wind up in jail. Haven't you been listening to what I've been saying?" he added sharply. "Your good uncle was living over his head. Maybe when he first used some of your funds he intended to put them back, but from what I've read a lot of smart boys took a licking in the stock market a while back. Maybe Grayson will tell you how it happened; I can only guess. He simply got in too deep. He could stay and face the music when your auditors turned up the discrepancies and maybe wind up with a few years in prison, or he could grab some more and run. But if that was his choice he had to do it before the fifteenth, right?"

He looked again at Grayson who seemed somehow to have shrunk inside his neat double-breasted suit. "How much? Come on, Grayson. You know that Kent and I are going to take you over to your place when we finish and count it anyway."

The fight had gone from Grayson and he moved his hands weakly in some gesture of hopelessness."

"You searched my place."

"I did."

"Something over three hundred thousand."

"Why?" Carol asked, some vestige of her disbelief still showing.

"He told you." Grayson tipped his head toward Fenner. "I got in over my head. There was no way I could get out in the time I had left. It wouldn't be the first time I'd taken my money and run. All those years in Europe. I knew I had a few good years left. I decided I'd rather be a "wanted" ex-patriot again with Mona than spend the next four or five years in a cell."

"Oh." The girl finally accepted the truth. She finally said, sounding as if she really didn't care: "Where were you going?"

"Panama first," Fenner said, and went on to tell about how his airline friend had checked the reservations for him. "Tonight on the ten-o'clock flight. That's why I wanted to get him over here while there was still time. You see, I wanted to establish a motive for murder and —"

This time it was Carter who interrupted. "Maybe I missed something coming in late like that. I'm still not sure I get it."

Fenner took the time to go over his points step by step. He explained how Browning must have picked Grayson's secretary's brains a little each time he slept with her.

"He had both sets of records — or copies of them — and he had to know what was going on. He wanted to collect big and he had to do it before next Tuesday. He put it to Grayson. Pay off or get turned in. How much did he hit you for, Grayson?"

"A hundred thousand at first. He said he was getting a hundred thousand as a settlement from Carol to make her divorce easier — he was trying to make her pay two. I didn't know about his committing Carol to Ufford but I know now that was how he hoped to get the extra payment —"

"You only knew you couldn't trust him," Fenner said. "You were afraid that even if you paid he might blow the whistle just for the hell of it. He was just the kind who could do it."

He turned to Carol. "Did your uncle come here often?"

"No."

"When was the last time?"

"Quite a while ago."

"A month? Two? Three?"

"Three or four, I'd say."

"Something like that," Grayson said.

"Okay."

Fenner stood up and stretched. Ignoring the others and his manners, he went over and fixed another drink, took a sip, came back, and sat down. He felt some satisfaction that his hypothesis concerning Grayson had been correct, but the feeling didn't last because he had one more step to take.

"That was you who held the gun on me at Browning's place—my taxi man can probably identify you."

"It was," Grayson said, his reply barely audible.

"How did you get a key?"

"My secretary had one. When I got a chance I slipped it off her key ring."

"And the gun?"

"I've had it for years."

"You put on a good show with that phony tough-talking voice and the routine of standing me against the wall and searching me for a gun, pretending to be surprised that I was a private detective. You knew who I was when I walked in."

"Yes, but I had to be sure you didn't have a gun, didn't I? I didn't know what else to do . . . I guess that closet didn't hold you for long, did it?" he added regretfully.

"A few seconds," Fenner said and brought his thoughts back into focus. "There's just one thing left that bothers me. That little .22 that killed Browning. Unless there's a hell of a lot I still don't know, there's only one person who could have used it. Two actually."

"Who, Jack?" Murdock said.

"Well, Carol, obviously now that Frank Quinn isn't here to give her an alibi. But since I can't figure any way she could have got hold of a gun the night Frank was shot,

I think she can be eliminated."

He paused to glance at Carter, studying the bearded, bespectacled face and trying to read the expression in the eyes.

"That leaves you, Sam. I admit I haven't much in the way of proof, but who else is there?"

21

For a long moment then the room was absolutely still. No one moved, no one seemed even to breathe. When the sounds came they made a strange chorus, reflecting not words but exclamations of surprise, doubt, and reproach. In the end it was Carter who made the first articulate reply. His grin showed through the beard and his tone was patronizing and contemptuous.

"You've got to be kidding, Jack. That's a little far out, isn't it? Even for you?"

Fenner matched the grin. "A little," he admitted. "And there's one thing that still bugs me. But facts are facts, right?"

"Always have been. *If* they're facts and not suppositions.'

"Right. So let's stick with that little .22 for a while, okay? Item one: You bought it for an extra gun and it's registered in your name. You made a hell of a fuss that first

317

night when we went over to talk to Frank Quinn, saying it was yours and the police could trace it—which I understand they did. You said if Carol wouldn't admit you gave it to her, things could be sticky.

"Item two: You were the only one, not counting Carol, who knew where that gun was kept. Either you or she—I can't remember for sure—told me that you told her not to leave the gun in her bedside table but to keep it close by the entryway."

He stood up, shifted his glass to his left hand, and moved over to the table just inside the living room. He glanced at the girl.

"Is this where you kept it?"

"Yes."

"The drawer was partway open when I found Browning."

He pointed to the ugly scar in the wall where the bullet had been removed by the police and not yet repaired. It was nearly head-high and slightly to his right as he stood there.

"Whoever Browning was aiming at when he got that one shot off had to be standing in this area and—"

318

"Wait a minute. Hold it!" There was derision in the tone, but Carter's grin was still fixed. "Slow down. Why am I the *only* one who knew where the gun was?"

"You told us that night out there with Frank Quinn that you gave it to Carol about six weeks ago. You just heard her say Grayson hadn't been here for months. When I was checking out Alan Hubbard, I found out he would take Carol out to dinner but he never came up when he brought her home. At least not while I was checking." He glanced at the girl. "Did he, at any time?"

"Never. I stopped asking him. The Puritan hang-up of his wouldn't let him compromise a married woman, not even his ex-wife."

"So who does that leave, Carter, that had any interest or motive for killing Browning?"

"Let's stick with the motive."

"Let's. But first we go back a couple or three years. Kent made a call to Los Angeles this afternoon and talked to a reporter who once worked for the *Courier*. He made some inquiries about you," he said and then, turning to the others, he related the information about Carter's gambling, the final big loss on the New Year's Day bowl games.

"Thirty-eight hundred bucks in the hole the first day of the new year and he knew what would happen if he didn't come up with it. It was a little too much, right, Sam? So you took off. That you finally wound up on the *Courier* and that Browning also had come here to live apparently was nothing but coincidence."

He paused for an answer and Carter confirmed his personal disaster, his voice indicating he still couldn't believe it.

"It couldn't happen," he said, "but it did. Four favorites. I had to give points. Biggest upsets of all times on the same day. There was no way I could pay off and I knew what would happen. They probably couldn't kill a newspaperman, but I'd be a hospital case some dark night and when I was released it could happen again. There was just one way I might get the money."

"A shylock?"

"Right. In fact a loan shark came around to see me. He could let me have the dough, but you know how the interest goes on that kind of loan. You never can pay off—no way. He had a proposition: he'd carry me so long as I used my job and contacts to keep the mob informed on any inside information I had or could get."

He shook his head, as though to dispel the picture his memory had just painted. "I may not be a lot of things," he said flatly, "but I am a damn good newspaperman. I wasn't about to peddle information to those bastards, so that night I called the office and said my father was seriously ill. I took my few hundred in savings and blew town while I still had my health."

Fenner said he didn't blame him because he understood how bad debts were handled. Then he said:

"But let's stick to Browning, hunh? He had a record as a wife beater and was finally sentenced. As a crime reporter you could know that. When he ran with the boss's dough from that used car lot a larceny warrant was issued and is still outstanding. That's something else you either knew or heard about. So since coincidence is a fact of life I say you knew who Browning was, and one fine day you saw him on the street or at the track—maybe a picture in the society page. You recognized him. You found out he was married to a woman with money, that he not only had a fat allowance but charge accounts until she cut him off."

Carter's answering grunt had a nasty sound. "That's sheer speculation and you know it."

"Not all of it, Sam," Fenner said, and went on to tell them about the information his Los Angeles colleague had supplied. "Browning's wife still lives out there. She never divorced him, never got a notice of action. If I could find that out with a long-distance call you could have done the same if you didn't already know it."

That statement brought an exclamation from the girl. "You mean George was never my husband? I was never legally married to him?"

"That's the way it looks from here."

"Balls!" Carter snorted. "Still speculation."

"It can be checked out," Fenner said. "And there's something else I think we can prove to substantiate every damn thing I've told you. What I mean, Sam, is that five-hundred-a-month payment you've been getting from Browning."

He glanced at Murdock, who sat at ease, dark eyes interested as he nodded approval. He looked at Grayson, who had also begun to show some interest. Talking now to Carol, he explained about the monthly checks her husband had written and made out to cash so that there would be no record of payment to anyone else. When he saw she understood, he continued to Carter.

"Those checks in themselves don't prove you got the money but when I turn what I have over to Homicide and they subpoena your bank account and get access to your safe-deposit box, if any, you'll have to explain why your recent income is so much in excess of your *Courier* salary, right?

"So I say you were collecting regularly, not being greedy or demanding more than Browning could pay. But that nice gravy was going to end on next Tuesday. Once Browning got his settlement from Carol he couldn't care less if she found out she was never really married to him. I know if it were me I'd hit him for one fat and final payment and close out the account. Isn't that what you did, Sam?"

"If I had, would I have killed him before I collected?"

"That," said Fenner, his smile reluctant but honest, "is what beats me. There has to be a reason because I know damn well you killed him, just like you conned Frank Quinn into taking a ride with you."

He swore under his breath then, good humor vanishing and a sudden cold and vindictive mood possessing him as he thought of his dead friend.

"They'll nail you, Sam. I think I've got more background evidence than the police have because I knew more in the beginning than they did, and I could work on personal angles that were not open to them. They may be sore for a little while, but if what I give them pays off they'll forget it, believe me."

"Fair enough." Carter stood up, still outwardly unperturbed. He still wore his topcoat and now with his hands in his pockets he tightened it round his hips. "It's been very interesting, but if you don't mind I'll get back to work. You can send the law around any time."

"I think I do mind," Fenner said. "Sit down, Sam!"

Carter gave him a hard, belligerent look, but something in Fenner's voice and his sudden change in manner was obvious even to him. He sat down, amber eyes narrowing and wary now behind the black-rimmed glasses.

"I've held out on Sergeant Gaynor too long as it is," Fenner added. "I'm going to make it easy for him this time." He hesitated, glanced at Murdock, and was reassured by his presence. "So"—he put his glass aside and came to his feet—"I'll just make my call and we'll all rest easy here until Joe shows up and collects you. It shouldn't take long."

He looked at Carol, whose hazel eyes reflected her bewilderment. "Okay with you, Carol? . . . Grayson? . . . Murdock?" Noticing some movement of Carter's, he added: "You don't object, Sam?"

Carter took a long visible breath and expelled it noisily, a new and almost embarrassed expression on his bewhiskered face.

"I'm afraid I do, Jack," he said and now there was a short-barreled gun in his right hand as it slipped from his pocket. "Maybe *you'd* better sit down."

Fenner eyed the gun with surprise and then respect. It had never occurred to him that Carter would be carrying a gun, but even as he berated himself for ignoring the possibility he found himself wondering if this was the weapon that had killed Frank Quinn.

Needing no further urging, he took his seat and, aware now that he still had a swallow or two left in his glass, he finished the drink. When he looked back at Carter he saw that the gun—he thought it might be a .32—was no longer pointed at anyone. Still in the other's right hand, the left had moved over so that it was cradled in both, the muzzle angled at the floor a few feet away.

"What's that for, Sam?" he said.

"Nothing drastic, I hope. Let's just say I think it will buy me a little time . . . I made a mistake," he added.

"Only one, Sam?" Murdock said evenly.

Carter ignored him. "If I'd used my

head," he said, as though talking to himself, "I could have taken the police investigation on Browning. But you kill a man—"

"Two men," Fenner said.

"—and the fear gets you," Carter finished. "Part abstract, part very real. Not conscience. With Browning, it was him or me, and he had the first shot. Fear, that's the thing. You think you're okay but you can't *know*. You can't get away from it. It's constant. I knew you were digging, and Kent's been through the routine before. I kept saying to myself, 'If one of these guys stumbles on something and corners you, either one can take you, Sam. The gun'll get you clear at least for a little while.' "

His shoulders had started to sag and he straightened them with a conscious effort.

"So, just to be sure, I brought it along." Then, as some new thought came to him, a curious smile took shape beneath the mustache. "And you know something. I guess it is going to buy me some time at that . . . Have you got a telephone in your bedroom, Carol?"

"Why, yes," she said, smooth brows

warping as she tried to follow the digression.

"Is it an extension of this one?"

"Yes."

Carter leaned forward, lifting the gun slightly. "Well, if you'll all stay put, I'll rip this one out before I go. That way I'll have two or three minutes start before you can find another one. You wouldn't be thinking about trying to jump me, would you, Jack?"

22

Again the room was still as Carter's glance moved from face to face. The question was rhetorical and required no answer, but as the silence started to build, Murdock broke it. Heretofore he had been content to let Fenner carry the ball with no more than an occasional comment; now he addressed Carter, his dark eyes in sharp focus now and his tone low and even.

"What did you mean, Sam, about your shooting Browning in self-defense? If that's the story you're going to give the D.A., why not try it on us and see how it sounds?"

Fenner took a small breath and leaned back, some sense of relief coming when he realized he was going to have help from a competent and respected source. He had been considering Carter's position for some time, and the gun, weighing the odds but making no decision until now.

Once before, many years ago now, he had jumped a man who held a gun on him. That time luck was with him and all he had to show for it was a scar — still noticeable when he took a shower — on his rib cage. But that had been part of his job. He'd been paid to take any reasonable chance. This was different. Amateurs with handguns were unpredictable. Alone in the room with Carter he might still have considered putting his skill and experience to a test, just for the hell of it. Here there were too many innocents who might get hit in a showdown.

Not this time, he thought. *No more of that for old Jack.*

And feeling satisfied with his decision for the moment, paying attention to Murdock's line of questioning, he heard Carter say:

"It happens to be true."

"How? You were making the demands, Sam. You wanted a big score and you had to get it some way before Browning collected his payments from Carol and Grayson and ran. It seems to me that he was the one who had the motive to kill."

"He did."

The simple statement brought another

330

silence. Murdock waited for the rest of it, dark glance still probing. When there was no elaboration he persisted.

"I don't get it. Are you saying he set you up here, making the date before he knew Carol had walked away from Ufford?"

"Right. The night before. He said he was ready to pay off."

"You both kept that date?" Fenner said.

"Right again. I came here right after I'd left your office that first night. Apparently he beat me to it. When he opened that outer door"—he pointed—"the gun you saw, the .38 you found by his body, was three inches from my belly. He invited me in. He stood here in the middle of the room and I knew what kind of pay-off he had in mind."

"He was just going to knock you off here and walk out, hoping to get away with it?"

"Not quite. He was a cagey bastard and the plan he had was pretty neat . . . You know about those threats I'd been getting warning me to kill my syndicate series?"

"I heard about them."

"Others actually saw them, three altogether. Of the two phone calls, one was overheard." He watched Murdock nod and said: "Well, why shouldn't I think they were legitimate? Not only that. You dig deep enough into the rackets like I did and you sort of expect them. It happened to me once before."

"Ohh—" Murdock's voice suggested the truth was beginning to come and Fenner was right with him. "You mean they were phony?"

"Browning made them. He told me so. If they found me some night in an alley or the back of a stolen car with a couple of slugs in my head, what else could the cops think but that it was another gang killing by a hired gun?

"And that was exactly what he intended to do. The hell of it was, I knew it could work. He was going to march me out of here and down to his car, with the gun in my back, and there wasn't a damn thing I could do about it until I remembered the little .22. It wasn't much of a chance but it was something if the gun was in that table where I'd last seen it. I sort of edged slightly in front of it and looked over my shoulder to plead a little and get his attention while I inched the drawer open."

He took a small breath and said: "When I got my hand on it I yanked it out and dropped sideways. I'm no athlete, but somehow I got turned round in mid-air before I hit on one knee. He fired late—you saw the bullet hole—and I got two quick ones off before he could aim again because the instant I shot I flattened for a third." He shrugged. "I didn't need it. It took him a while to fold but he must have been paralyzed because he couldn't lift his gun.

"At first I was going to take the .22 and get rid of it," he said. "But I knew Carol would be questioned when the police located her. The autopsy would show Browning had been killed by .22 slugs. Before they finished with her I knew she'd tell the truth about the gun and where she got it. I'd still get tied in. By leaving it and admitting certain facts, I gambled that the police would reason that no one in his right mind would use a murder gun and leave it behind to be traced to him. I thought I knew how their minds worked and for once I was right."

He stood up, holding his revolver waist high, and started backing toward the telephone. Fenner, wanting to hold his attention as long as he could and hoping he would get careless, told him to wait a minute and turned to Grayson.

"How does it sound to you, counselor? Would his story add up to self-defense?"

Grayson had to rouse himself. He had been sitting there mute and disinterested for so long he had to make a conscious effort to bring his thoughts to bear on the question. It took him a while, but he finally came up with an answer.

"It's possible. At the worst I think a deal could be made for manslaughter. The gun Browning had and the hole in the wall would support it."

Carter had sidled past Grayson as the lawyer gave his opinion and Murdock said:

"So why run, Sam? Why not get yourself a good criminal lawyer and let him defend you. You must have a pretty fair sockful if you saved any of that five hundred a month you've been collecting all this time."

"I might just do that, Kent. But I need a little time. And then" — he held out the gun — "there's this."

That simple statement set up new forces in Fenner's brain, and now he was thinking about Frank Quinn and how he had been killed because, for some reason known only to him, Quinn had failed to mention Carter's name in the report he gave Fenner that night in his car. The interest he'd had in Carter's explanation turned now to resentment and some deep-seated desire to see the reporter pay in some more suitable way.

"I take it you used *that* gun on Frank Quinn," he said, his voice tight but controlled. "Why the hell didn't he tell us he'd seen you? I can understand his weakness in wanting to blackmail Carol once he'd found out she was the hippie he'd seen. Carol had money. She'd pay for a solid alibi. You didn't know about that, Sam?"

Carter shook his head and his expression told Fenner it was the truth so he took time out to explain what Quinn had done. When he finished he said:

"I can't figure Frank holding out for the petty pay-off he'd get from you."

Carter's thin grin had come back. He shook his head. "You want some answer from me, Jack, forget it. For the record, and in front of witnesses, all I know about what happened to Quinn is what you told me the noon they found his body."

"You could discuss a hypothetical case." Fenner looked at Grayson who had recovered and seemed more interested, more like himself. "Admission on a purely hypothetical situation could not be used as evidence regardless of witnesses, could it?"

"Not if it was understood by those present that it was hypothetical and nothing more," Grayson said.

Fenner asked the room at large if it was agreed that what followed would be hypothetical. When he got the required nods, he turned once more to Carter.

"Okay, Sam. Say a well-known reporter is seen by a reliable witness coming out of a building where a murder has been recently committed. The reporter has been there long enough to do the job and at approximately the right time. The witness reports to the one who hired him to stakeout that apartment. He states that three people called who could have been involved but fails to mention the reporter. Why?"

"Still answering hypothetically," Carter

said, "I think the fact that this reporter was looking right at the witness when he gave his evidence may have influenced him. The witness knew this man confronting him could have done the job, but because of this reporter's reputation he might be hesitant to put the finger on him without giving the reporter a chance to explain.

"I don't think this witness had blackmail in mind at the moment. He just wanted to give the reporter the benefit of the doubt. A little later, still concerned, he collects big to give this third person an alibi. He then phones the reporter and makes a date. The reporter, expecting the worst and fearing blackmail he could not possibly pay, takes a gun—"

"Why?" Murdock said.

"Because he's scared stiff. By that time the sweat is cold on his spine and he can't get rid of the fear that has been with him constantly all those hours since he killed the first man, even though that was in self-defense. The guilt is there. All his moral training tells him to stop, look, and listen, but he's thinking of a life sentence, maybe, and he knows he can never be sure that the witness won't change his mind and testify against him. So the fears overwhelm him and with it comes a sort of helpless compulsion that finally says, 'Don't take a chance, pull the trigger while you can —' "

He stopped suddenly, out of breath as the words trailed off. He seemed to shake himself unconsciously like someone coming out of a trance or an actor who has completed satisfactorily the climax of a play. He straightened his shoulders and looked at Fenner.

"I guess that's about the only answer I could honestly give to a hypothetical question like that. Just remember that that's what it is, too. Strictly hypothetical.

Fenner, alert and watchful as he listened, believed what he had heard. It fitted nicely with his own estimate of the man he had known as Frank Quinn. A nice guy but weak, basically kind, not wanting to put anyone on the spot until he had all the facts. This time, giving the other fellow the benefit of the doubt before he committed himself had cost him his life.

And Carter was going to get away with it if he got rid of that gun. It was the only solid evidence that could be conclusive. There was a chance that if he, Fenner, reached a telephone quickly and an alert police patrol car happened to be in the neighborhood, Carter could be picked up before he could dispose of the gun. Unfortunately the likelihood of such a happy combination of circumstances was remote.

What galled him as such thoughts came to him was that he could do nothing about it. Carter and that gun were altogether too far away, not only from him but from Murdock. Still, he shifted his weight slightly and planted his feet in case the opportunity came. Because he knew somehow that he could break his earlier resolve not to go up against the gun if he honestly thought the odds were right.

Then, as he sat there in his angry impotence, something happened that seemed to prove that there were occasions when justice prevailed.

The catalyst came from the most unlikely source and with such total unexpectedness that Fenner, for all his agility and experience, was left flat-footed and helpless. For Carter, having passed in front of

Grayson, shifted the gun to his left hand to fumble with his right for the telephone cord. When he missed it the first time, he turned his head for a second to locate it.

At that same instant a revitalized Grayson, no more than four feet away, lunged, both hands outstretched like a man grabbing for a grapefruit.

The curled fingers clamped tight on the half-extended wrist. The revolver, twisted downward in that first instant, exploded harmlessly into the floor as Grayson's body momentum jerked the unsuspecting Carter off balance. The yank and the leverage were as good as a judo hold, and Carter went down hard with the older man on top of him. That left the gun arm stiffly extended to one side and Murdock, who was closer, sprung from his chair, took one long stride, and stomped a shoe hard on that wrist.

Carter yelped. The gun slipped from nerveless fingers and Murdock picked it up and stepped back. Grayson rolled free and came to one knee, puffing hard as he pushed to his feet.

Later, when Fenner had a chance to think about it, he wondered just what had motivated Grayson's gamble, not that much risk was involved under the circumstances. It could have been some thought that his act might serve to improve his own chances of leniency when his crime was considered; he may have wanted to show his niece that he could also do the right thing when given a chance; perhaps it was nothing more than a spontaneous impulse prompted by some deep-seated desire to see justice triumph.

Whatever the reason he had succeeded in doing what no one else in the room had been able to do and Fenner, taking the gun Murdock offered, voiced his approval.

"Nice work, Grayson. Thanks for doing my job for me."

By this time Carter was on his feet and his bespectacled eyes were slits of hate as he turned on Grayson.

"You miserable, sneaky bastard!" he said, his voice high, hoarse, and vicious. "Why couldn't you give me a chance? I'd have turned myself in when the time came."

"For Browning maybe," Fenner said, "but not for Frank Quinn. You should have faced up to it that first night."

Carter glared at him, his face gray and

twisted. "You're not going to keep me here," he said, his voice breaking under the strain.

"Grayson!" Fenner had to raise his voice to get the man's attention. "Go over and sit by your niece."

Grayson looked at him then, as though just beginning to understand where he was and what had happened. He seemed to move in great bewilderment as he glanced about, like a man still unable to believe what he had done.

Carter repeated his statement.

"I'm walking out of here, do you hear me? Use the gun if you want. Go ahead, shoot me in the back. That'd be better than the death sentence."

He started to brush past on his way to the door and Fenner reached out, grabbed an arm, and spun him about.

"No, you're not, Sambo. You try it and Murdock and I will break both your arms."

He spoke softly but with authority because he had already decided how to handle the situation. When Carter hesitated he put his palm flat against the reporter's chest and gave a quick, hard push that tipped him backward off balance.

"Don't make me lean on you, Sam. I'd love that. I really would." He pushed again, crowding now as Carter regained his balance, his voice tight and cold and menacing. "You got careless and you're stuck with it. The death penalty is academic anyway these days. Since when have you read or heard of any killer being put to death? . . . Right there!" he added, indicating a chair. "Now sit down and shut up!"

The flat and pointed logic of the words, the realization that the odds had finally caught up with him, apparently got through to Carter's basic intelligence. For right then his shoulders sagged and his defiance oozed away. There was still some sort of incredulous bewilderment showing in his amber eyes, but he shrugged hopelessly, glanced once more at the gun in Fenner's hand, groped for the chair behind him, and dropped heavily into it.

Fenner stuck the gun in his belt and buttoned his jacket. Over on the divan Grayson cleared his throat.

"Before you call the police," he said

hesitantly, "I'd like to know what happens to me?"

Fenner shrugged and nodded toward the girl, who seemed not to have moved in the last half hour. Her face remained composed but still held a concerned and wide-eyed look.

"That's up to Carol, isn't it? As a guess I'd say it might depend on how much more beside that three hundred grand you'd stolen. *Is* it much?"

"No."

"Well, then" — Fenner tipped one hand and examined the girl — "why not give her a little time to think it over? She's admitted that she's a spoiled, willful, demanding young woman." He gave her a slow wink. "Right, Carol?"

"Right," she said and made a face at him, her good humor returning.

"But not, I think, vindictive. So maybe, when you've given her your accounting, assuming you haven't clipped her too much, she might be compassionate enough to let it go at that and fire you. Then you and friend Mona can take it from there and be thankful you don't spend two or three years in or on the prison farm. But, as I said, that's up to Carol . . . I've got to call Sergeant Gaynor sometime," he said to Murdock.

"And I," Murdock said amiably, "will call the *Courier*."

"That's right. You're entitled to a beat."

Murdock glanced at his watch and grunted. "I'm afraid it won't be much of a beat at this hour. Too early . . . however, it's possible," he added cheerfully, "that the *Courier* coverage may be just a bit more comprehensive than the opposition."

Fenner, still thinking about his own problem, said: "There'll have to be a session, probably an extended one, with Gaynor and some assistant D.A."

"All of us?" Carol asked with some dismay.

Fenner reassured her. "Just me and old Sam for starters."

"You going to get Gaynor up here?" Murdock asked.

"No."

"Why not? Gaynor can get filled in and pick up Sam —"

"You're forgetting that three hundred thousand bucks, plus, aren't you?"

345

Murdock studied him, head tipping slightly and a grin beginning to show. "Now that you remind me, I am."

"So what I suggest is that you go to Grayson's place, with his keys, pick up a very heavy pigskin suitcase in his bedroom closet and bring it back here. Meanwhile Sam and I will pay headquarters a visit."

"I can stay here, Jack?" Carol said hopefully.

"You can. You can comfort your attorney until we get back. Have some sandwiches sent up. Play chess or a few hands of gin . . . You, Grayson, stay put, you understand?"

"Yes," Grayson said. "Naturally. Of course."

"Be nice to her, con her a little. Maybe she'll let you off the hook . . . While you're waiting you might want to call your girl friend and tell her to go and get a refund on those two tickets to Panama you won't be using tonight."

To Murdock he added: "You want to call your paper and tell your editor I'm bringing Carter in? Then go get the loot, hunh? It's only five minutes from here. When you get back maybe you'd better hang around to keep an eye on Grayson. I'll be back, I hope . . . Come on, Sam. You know your rights. You can call your attorney after we see Joe Gaynor."

He stopped in front of the two steps to glance at the girl and out of nowhere this new thought came to him.

"Oh, yeah," he said. "Why not give Alan Hubbard a ring? He'd like to know you're okay. You might ask him to stop by for a drink." He winked again. "If you tell him there'll be a chaperone this time he might even come."

She stuck her tongue out at him like a little girl but her hazel eyes were shining.

"Maybe I will, smarty."

Her reaction pleased him and it was not until he was in the foyer getting his coat that he realized Murdock was right behind him.

"Aren't you going to make your call?"

"In a few minutes." Murdock reached for his coat. "You're doing your job, let me do mine . . . I'm a photographer, remember?" he added with a small dry smile. "I've got an old Graphic in the trunk of my car I've been hauling around with me for twenty years. Sometimes I use it, like now. Before you take Sam away I want a shot of both of you."

Fenner gaped at him. "Oh, no! Jesus, Kent!" he said, both shocked and dismayed. "Gaynor is going to be sore enough at me as it is. I'm in trouble, man."

You won't be after the *Courier* prints my pix. With the public knowing that Jack Fenner, Esquire, Private Investigator, is the one who brought the killer in, the D.A.'s office can't push you too hard without getting the *Courier* on its back . . . Come on, quit crabbing."

For a moment more, as Fenner absorbed the words, he seemed unconvinced. Then the soundness of such reasoning became apparent and he nodded, reminded again that in a sticky situation Murdock generally came up with something that was soundly conceived.

"Okay, buddy boy," he said. "I guess you're entitled to a picture at that."

Out on the sidewalk he stood with one

hand on Carter's arm. The reporter, a dejected but unprotesting figure, stood docilely while Murdock went to his car and came back with the camera. When he had adjusted shutter and focus he said:

"Okay, Jackson, look intelligent . . . You, Sam! Get the chin up a little. You gambled and lost and you're stuck with it. But as a loyal *Courier* man and a good reporter, you're not going to cop out now when we have a chance for an exclusive."

The burst of light made Fenner blink and then he remembered something else. The fact that Carter had heretofore offered no resistance did not mean he might not try something if given the chance. He had no intention of using the gun in his belt at any time but, aware of the difficulties in driving with never more than one hand free, he asked Murdock to flag the next taxi that came along.

While he stood there holding Carter's arm as Murdock stepped out into the street, and before his thoughts moved on, there was a brief moment when he allowed himself the luxury of feeling rather pleased with the way things had worked out. The fact that he had put out considerable expense money with nothing more than what was probably a worthless check in his pocket to show for it suddenly seemed not to matter. He hoped Frank Quinn would approve.